SHAPESHIFTING

Michelle Ross

STILL
HOUSE
PRESS

All inquiries may be directed to:
    Stillhouse Press
    4400 University Drive, 3E4
    Fairfax, VA 22030
    www.stillhousepress.org

Stillhouse Press is an independent, student and alumni-run
nonprofit press based out of Northern Virginia and established in
collaboration with the Fall for the Book festival.

Cover image: Meghan Pinsonneault

Library of Congress Control Number: 2021935409
ISBN-13: 978-1-945233-10-4

AFTER PANGAEA

My husband was too busy proselytizing to do his part to secure Joey a slot in next fall's kindergarten class at the Montessori. This meant I would be camping five nights straight in a friend's metal mastodon of a van, which I'd borrowed because the back is carpeted and roomy enough to spread out a sleeping bag and blankets. Because I was still breastfeeding, I'd be burrowing in that hamster's nest with our four-month-old daughter.

"Stay home tonight and park in front of the school in the morning. Make it four nights. Or heck, wait until Tuesday. Isn't Wednesday when the line started last year?" My husband, Pete, a.k.a "The Daddy Sage," said this while trimming his nose hairs over my sink basin because his was clogged, and neither of us (me) had gotten around to de-clogging it.

"Tuesday," I said.

Two years ago, the queue for securing your kid a kindergarten slot started on Wednesday. Last year, the first vehicle, an RV, arrived by Tuesday morning. I drove past it as I dropped Joey off at the Montessori's preschool. (No queueing to get your kid into preschool because preschool isn't paid for by taxpayer dollars.) In the short time it took to walk Joey to his classroom and get back into the car, three more vehicles had manifested along the street behind the RV.

Weeks now, I'd been reminding Pete the queue began on Tuesday morning last year, which meant you could damn well be sure this year's queue would start up by Monday at the latest, and which was why I planned to be out there tonight, Sunday; and because I knew I probably wasn't the only one thinking along these lines, I'd fully loaded the van with clothes, bedding, snacks, books, and human waste supplies yesterday afternoon before driving out to the school last night just to be sure the line hadn't begun already.

Pete was preoccupied, though. Two or three nights a week now he was attending gatherings in the living rooms of his followers—hence the grooming, hence the clogged sink. Whereas before he'd trimmed his facial hair maybe once or twice a month, now stubby clumps of hair seemed to fall in the sink at the rate of the shed exoskeletons of cicadas from trees all over town last summer.

Two months ago, only strangers believed my husband was some kind of parenting messiah. Pete had been at least a touch incredulous. "Can you believe it? Me?"

No, I could not, I told him.

The evening he told me about it, he'd read me these people's comments on his social media feed and on his blog as I stirred chicken and broccoli in a wok, as I ordered the hard-to-find oven light bulb replacement over the internet, as I baked brownies for Joey's class party. After finishing almost an entire bottle of wine on his own, he was still reading comments, still marveling. His eyes bloomed and swirled like water when you drop in a tablet of Easter egg dye.

I only half listened. I figured that knowing too much about this business between Pete and his followers would be to our marriage like knowing too much about the life of the chicken on my plate before I ate it. If I was going to eat that chicken, then I needed to be blissfully ignorant.

Pete's first words the following morning were "Maybe they see something I don't."

"The point is they think *you* see something," I said.

Now Pete eyed me in the mirror. "Who cares if someone starts the registration queue tonight? Are there really so few kindergarten slots available that it can't wait until tomorrow morning?"

I said, "*You* tell *me* how many kindergarten openings there are."

Pete groaned. At least he showed enough good sense to be slightly embarrassed by the situation he'd not diffused when he still had the chance, I told myself. But I wondered if he was embarrassed *only* because I contradicted his followers' narrative. That is, if I too believed my husband was something extraordinary, would he be happy to play that part for me, as well?

I said, "We don't know how many kindergarten openings there are. That's why we can't take our chances."

Rumor was the school hadn't turned anybody away in several years. Everyone who camped out got in. But I knew it hadn't always been that way. When my friend Natasha slept in her station wagon for a mere night five years ago, before the camp-out thing got insane, a bunch of families got waitlisted. If the school had a lot of sibling enrollments the next fall, then there'd be fewer openings.

I picked up the Oregon State T-shirt Pete had left on the floor by his side of the bed and tossed it into the laundry basket. I said, "I'll keep the baby in the van tonight, but as soon as your thing is over, you need to come get Joey. I'm not getting my kid ready for school in a van. Plus, he kicks."

Pete smirked.

"What?" I said.

"You're being pretty militant about this camp-out thing. You're so competitive."

I assured my husband my militancy was purely tactical. The prospect of camping out four nights in a van with an infant only to *not* get Joey in was too miserable to leave to chance. Better to camp five nights. Better to be first in line. Better to be certain.

*

When I pulled the van onto the side of the road across from Joey's school, a black SUV was already parked there in the dark. Sweet vindication. I couldn't wait to text Pete that I was right about the queue beginning tonight.

I knew from the days of dropping Joey off and picking him up that there wasn't a lot of space between the road and the yard of the people who lived directly across from the school. Joey's school was located in a residential area. The houses were like hotels compared to our little house. The yard directly across the street from the school was bordered by pretty vines and shrubs and flowers, and I tried to wedge the van into that tight space without doing damage to the greenery.

I'd barely turned off the ignition when a thick guy in a camouflage jacket tapped on my window. A black knit cap was pulled low over his forehead. He squinted at me as he asked me to write my name in slot #2 on a list he'd made on a yellow legal pad. Then he gave me a sheet of paper with a huge number "2" in black marker.

Accepting that #2 as big as my hand, I felt a little giddy. Perhaps Pete hadn't been entirely wrong about the competitive nature of this endeavor.

"Keep your number visible in your windshield at all times," he said. "Rule is you can leave for up to twenty minutes without losing your place in line. Just don't go taking off too often."

"You with the school?" I didn't recognize him from the office, and I knew full well he wasn't one of the teachers.

"I'm Gabriel. I'm number one," he said.

Joey said, "Do you have a business card?" He collected business cards in a binder meant for Pokémon cards or baseball cards, or back in my day, Garbage Pail Kid cards.

He'd been collecting the cards from coffee shop bulletin boards for nearly a year. Once, he'd tried to fish out a fistful from a bowl for a gift card raffle at my hair salon.

"No," was all Gabriel said, but he squinted at me again before turning away.

As soon as Gabriel disappeared into the dark from which he'd come, Joey said he needed to use the bathroom.

"Pee?" I said, hopeful.

He nodded.

"I'll help you use one of the pee bags," I told him.

"I don't like those," he said.

"I don't, either, but they're better than having to drive around looking for a bathroom every half hour, and you heard the guy, if we leave too often, we lose our spot. You don't want to have to go to a different school next year, without your friends, do you?"

"That man will see," he said.

I looked out the window at the SUV. In this dark, I could barely make out my own dashboard. No streetlights allowed in our town's residential areas—an effort to curb light pollution for stargazing.

"It's dark, and your sister's asleep. The only person who can see you is me."

I unraveled the white bag with the plastic top. Joey whined.

"Don't you wake your sister," I said. "I'll hold the bag with my eyes closed. Just make sure you put your penis all the way in, so you don't spill, OK?"

Holding that bag, I thought, See, Pete, *this* is devotion to your children. Pete would have opened the door of the van and told Joey to pee into the homeowners' shrubs like a dog.

When Joey was done, I held the bag upright, waiting for the chemical beads to turn my son's urine into non-spilling gel.

Joey said, "I want to sleep in the van, too."

"If you sleep in the van, you have to pee in one of these every time you need to go to the bathroom in the night," I said. "Also, you can't because you have school in the morning."

Joey pointed to the window next to the baby. I looked for the man from the SUV, Gabriel, #1.

Joey said, "Slug."

"Inside or outside?"

"Inside. How did it get in here?"

"I don't know," I said. The same way this landscape gets into everything, I thought. When I'd first moved to Oregon with Pete a year before I got pregnant, I'd felt itchy just looking at all this green. Pete took me hiking in some woods he'd hiked since he was a kid, and damn if even the rocks weren't green, covered in thick, curly lichen that resembled pubic hair. Those woods were dank, too. "It's like we're hiking the folds of some green giantess's labia," I'd said. On the rural backroads we took home, green stuff grew from the damn potholes. I'd lived all my life up until then in the desert. Dirt and scrubby, prickly things as far as the eye could see. Wildflowers sprouting from potholes unsettled me. It went against my sense of the natural order of things. Life wasn't supposed to be so easy.

I got out of the car, quietly opened the passenger door behind me, and scraped the slug off the window with the piece of paper with the #2 on it. Other than the books I'd brought, it was the only paper I had. Good thing Gabriel beat me here. He was much better prepared.

"What did you do to the slug?" Joey said when I was back in the driver's seat.

"I placed it gently on the ground," I lied.

"If you're lying about that slug, will Daddy know it?" he said. "Would he sense it?"

This was my own damn fault for teasing Pete in front of our son. All Pete had ever said to Joey about those meetings was that they were kind of like Joey's and his friend Lee's spy club.

"Your Daddy isn't all-knowing. I was kidding him," I said.

"But those people," he said. "They think he's important."

Pete and Joey and the baby and I had been out having breakfast at a local café a few weeks back and this couple at another table kept looking at us, whispering. The woman's spiky, bleached-blonde hair had looked like a patch of dead grass. Her eyes had buzzed. The man's right foot was where his nervous energy went. I fantasized duct-taping that spastic foot to the floor. They were my first and only glimpse of the sort of people who attended the living-room gatherings organized for the express purpose of hearing my husband speak, an act of my husband's that seemed about as precious to me as his trimming his nose hair. When Pete waved, the couple promptly bombarded our table. "Transformed" was one of the actual words to come out of the woman's mouth as she gazed adoringly at my husband.

In the car, Joey had wanted to know what it was Pete had said to them. He eyed his father with gluey awe. Those sticky, stifling, yet sweet days of being my son's everything were gone. Joey had stopped looking at me like that even before Sophia was born, but the separation had become starker since her birth. Whereas once we'd been as fused together as Pangaea, now Joey was Australia to my Antarctica.

Before Pete could answer, I said those people were creepy, and I didn't like that they saw us with Pete, that they now knew who we were. Pete dismissed my concern. He said those people were parents, too, as if that proved something about their sanity. (Also, out on a Saturday morning without kids in tow? I was skeptical about the existence of these kids.) He told me to "chill out," a phrase that has the opposite effect on my internal temperature.

In the van, I said to Joey, "Your daddy's no better than the rest of us."

Joey said nothing, but he refused to lay in the back of the van with me. He insisted the back seat was more comfortable.

*

In the morning, I watched for Pete's car. When I spotted it, I got out of the van and waited for Pete at the parking lot exit.

The first thing he said through the rolled-down window was "Where's Sophia?"

"In the van," I said. "She's asleep. She's exhausted."

"I already told you I'm sorry. I don't know what more to say."

Another car was queued behind Pete's now. The driver was a guy I'd talked to briefly at a welcoming event when we first enrolled Joey in the preschool a year and a half ago. He was one of those overly symmetrical people, like he'd been popped out of a mold. At that event, he'd gone on about how his three-year-old, River, wasn't going to be challenged enough by regular schools. River was Joey's age, but River had an older sister in the upper elementary, so River's pompous dad didn't have to sleep in a van for a week like an animal. He had a free pass. His eyes on me from inside his windshield, I became aware of how frumpy I must look in my scraggly sweatshirt and maternity jeans (nobody tells you you'll continue to look pregnant for months after giving birth).

"I'll park and come over," Pete said.

The van was now one among fifteen vehicles parked along either side of the street outside the school.

I opened the door to find Sophia was crying. Over my shoulder, Pete said, "Guess she's not asleep anymore."

Early that morning, snuggled in the back of the van with our baby, despite my anger over Pete's late arrival last night, I'd wished he were in the van with me, his body curled around mine. But now I turned, and though the man standing before me was the same man, he was also not the same man. Pete was a kaleidoscope. Sometimes, though mostly just in my imagination these days, the flecks fell into a beautiful pattern. Other times, like now, like nearly every time I saw him in the flesh, the flecks fell into a less flattering pattern, and I wished I could shake them up and try again.

Some of the parents were fraternizing on the side of the road with Starbucks cups in their hands. You could tell from a quick glance who was at the front of the line and who'd arrived this morning. The new arrivals looked fresher—their hair clean, faces bright. But the haggard people had assurance that no amount of overpriced coffee could compete with.

Pete whispered, "So something happened last night."

"Flat tire? Held up by a train?" I said. When he'd arrived at eleven, neither of us had spoken. I'd simply shaken my head as he carried Joey's limp body out of the backseat of the van.

"No, I mean at the meeting," Pete said.

I passed Sophia to him, and he took her with a look of surprise, as though a stranger had just handed him their baby.

I waited.

"Aren't you going to ask me what?"

"Aren't you going to tell me regardless?"

He lowered his voice further. "This one guy called me, 'Our Father.' He said it kind of jokingly, but it caught on. That's what they're calling me now on social media. 'Our Father,' Capital 'o,' capital 'f.'"

I stared at Pete.

I thought about my husband's exhibitionism—the way he'd pressed me to have sex on an apartment fire escape one time. Another time: in a car in a Taco Bell parking lot. How he had once whispered in my ear while my sister was sleeping on our fold-out sofa bed, "Want your sister to hear you come?" (My answer: nope.)

Then I thought about his slovenliness. Bits of paper napkins often got stuck on the stubble on his upper lip when he wiped his mouth. He did the dishes in his boxer briefs, and his T-shirt would get inadvertently tucked into his underwear.

"Isn't that blasphemous?" I said.

When I first started dating Pete, my friend Annie had said, "A churchgoer? I give this one a month max." Later, when I'd told her he sometimes voted Republican, she'd choked on her latté. "What the fuck, Tia?" she'd said. I'd said, "The sex is really hot." When we got engaged, Annie said, "What are you going to do when you guys have kids and Pete wants to get them baptized or some shit?" I told her Pete wasn't Baptist, that he was Unitarian or something. Another thing I'd chosen not to know much about. Annie had just stared at me.

Pete said, "It's a play on words. Tongue-in-cheek. They don't mean it disrespectfully. Anyway, so they think I should retitle my blog *Our Father*."

I snatched Sophia, who had quieted in his arms, back from him.

I used to think of Pete and me as being something like James Carville and Mary Matalin. Yeah, we were from opposite sides of the spectrum, but something about us made sense. Now I wondered if we were more absurd than that, like a page from one of Joey's books: an octopus in love with a glove.

I said, "That doesn't even make sense. You can't refer to yourself with the pronoun 'our.'"

Pete said, "You're always so literal. The point is people are interested in what I have to say. I'm doing some good in the world."

"Oh, Pete," I said.

Preposterously, Pete looked wounded. "You don't think I'm helping people?"

I said, "If you want to help people, how about starting with your family? I'm sleeping in a fucking van with an infant. The van smells like dirty diapers because it, in fact, contains a garbage bag of dirty diapers and my and our son's urine. The van is cold at night, and I worry our daughter may freeze to death."

"I can't tonight," Pete said. "I'm really, really sorry, and I know I owe you big time, but I can't. I committed to tonight's meeting a few weeks ago, and I have work in the morning. But I'll relieve you of the garbage. And Lorna can watch the kids this evening, right? Wasn't it only Sunday that she had plans? That'll give you a break."

"I work, too," I said.

"But you're working part-time from home right now. You can make it up this weekend."

"Lorna is expensive. We're saving money, remember?"

"I'm calling Lorna," he said. "I'll come get the kids from you at 4:30. I'll bring you dinner. I'll bring you the pump. I'll bring you wine if you want it. Just text me."

With that, my husband-turned-sage-turned-Our-Father walked away, apparently having forgotten his promise to relieve me of the bag of human waste.

*

While I breastfed the baby with the window down, I listened to #6 in line, a guy named Zane, tell Gabriel, #1, about how last night some guy came out of his house and yelled at him for shining his headlights on the man's kid's bedroom window. "I couldn't have had the lights on for more than a minute. Dude nearly lost his shit," Zane said between puffs of a cigarette. Zane must have been the one who'd pulled up not so long before Pete showed up last night. The headlights had lit my wristwatch so I could see just how late Pete was. By my count, those headlights had been on for at least three minutes.

Zane wore a perpetual smirk on his face. He reminded me of the guys I'd known in high school so many years ago. Guys who acted like they thought they could charm squirrels into giving them their buried nuts. Gabriel didn't smile back at Zane. He let Zane's smirk fly past him and crash into the earth like a ball he couldn't be bothered to catch and return. That knit hat was still on Gabriel's head, even though at noon it was sunny and in the low seventies.

Joey was probably on the school's covered patio eating lunch about now. I wondered what Pete had put in Joey's lunch box. I pictured tins stuffed with cereal, popcorn, and pretzels. As much as Pete bitched if I gave Joey a second cookie after dinner, leave meal prep to him, and there wasn't a vegetable in sight. Too much work, all that washing and chopping. Pete wouldn't even slice an apple.

Zane said, "I was tempted to give the guy shit right back, but my wife would kill me if I lost our spot in line because I got hauled off by the cops." He laughed.

At the end-of-school party the previous spring, Pete's eyes had sharpened to spikes when a kid barely older than Joey cut us in the food line. I'd squeezed Pete's arm as his mouth opened. "Let it go," I'd said. Clearly the kid hadn't understood we were in line. What was the point in scolding him? When, a few minutes later, the line moved ahead as the kid was in a squat, tying his shoelaces, we stepped around him. I wasn't in support of my husband barraging a seven-year-old for obliviously cutting a burger line, but I wasn't keen on saving the line-cutter's spot, either. When the kid stood again, he came around us, said earnestly, "I was in front of you." Pete gave the kid a menacing look. "Believe me, I know all about it."

It struck me that Pete was kind of like Zane. He had no empathy for anyone else's kid. But if anyone dare fuck with his kid, whether or not Joey deserved it, Pete would give them hell.

Defending Joey was, in fact, how this whole sage-turned-Our-Father business had started in the first place. Because I couldn't get much work done at home during the day with the baby, Pete usually took the kids in the late afternoons. Sometimes they went on walks through the neighborhood or to the playground, sometimes to the indoor play area at the mall. He started documenting his afternoons with the kids and posting blog links on social media. He shared anecdotes and riffed on what bugged him about how other people treated our children. What set everything in motion was some guy in the mall grabbing Joey by the shoulder because Joey had run in front of his elderly mother. The guy told Joey to watch where he was going so he didn't hurt someone, which was fair enough, I pointed out, when Pete relayed the story. But Pete fixated on the nerve of this man laying a hand on Joey. I conceded that I didn't exactly like that the man had put his hand on our son, but I thought Pete's outrage was overblown. Not the people who followed him on social media. Pete, a guy who struggles to use apostrophes correctly, wrote a manifesto about parenting in a world in which everyone on the street feels justified in telling you how to raise your kids when the truth was that only you knew what was best for your kids. Something about the way Pete talked about his knowing resonated with his audience or got lost in translation, I wasn't sure which. Add to that the fact that my husband is a man easily flattered and, voilà, you had the ingredients for a cult.

The insanity of people publicly referring to Pete as Our Father was new, but the part where people praised the heck out of Pete for being a good father was tiringly familiar. Me, on the other hand, I was just doing what I was supposed to do, what I was made for.

When I complained about this to Pete, he acted unawares. "What do you mean? I've heard people compliment you on your mothering," he'd say.

"But not with the same enthusiasm and awe. Not in an oh-my-god-praise-Jesus sort of way," I'd say.

Then one day Pete said, "Maybe that's because you're not that devoted a mother."

"Excuse me?" I said. This was when I was about seven or eight months pregnant with Sophia, when she'd shift sometimes so that the shape of her bones visibly deformed my abdomen, making my body look like one of those dig-your-own-fossils kits Joey liked so much.

"I just mean you're not loyal to the degree that I am. Like if some kid picks on Joey, the first words out of your mouth concern whether Joey did anything to warrant the picking."

"So?" I said.

"I don't think like that. I don't assume the worst of my kid."

"I don't, either, but what if he was accused of rape or something? Would you assume he's innocent and that the accuser was a liar?"

"See, that's what I'm talking about. You can imagine all these scenarios in which you wouldn't be on our child's side," Pete said.

*

After two nights and two days in the van, I told Pete when he showed up Tuesday afternoon that if he didn't at least hang out in the van for a few hours while I went home to shower, I'd divorce him.

I didn't even realize how bad Sophia and I smelled until I got out of the shower and the odor of my dirty infant hit me fresh. I bathed her in the sink for nearly twenty minutes.

After toweling her off, I lay down next to Sophia on her bunny blanket.

"I'm so tired," I said to her.

If Joey hadn't been back at the van with Pete, I would have left Pete there for the night. I cursed myself for not making

Joey come home with me. But Joey had wanted to stay with Pete, and I'd been relieved to have one less human to care for, especially the child who made it so clear day after day that his loyalty belonged to his father.

When I returned to the van, Joey was sitting in it alone, flipping through his business-card binder.

"Where's your daddy?" I asked.

Joey pointed toward a little green tent at the edge of someone's property. A group of five men sat in front of it, including Gabriel, Zane, and my husband. They were drinking beer. Pete was gesticulating with his free hand. Whatever he was saying, his audience was laughing, even Gabriel.

I honked the horn. The men turned. Pete put up a hand. He kept right on talking.

When he returned to the van, I said, "If I'd known you'd be having such a good time, I would have stayed home a while longer. Taken a nap on the bed."

"Oh, I was just hanging out. Being social," he said.

The only fellow camper I'd spoken to was Gabriel, the night he handed me the sheet of paper with the #2 on it. But I didn't say this. My being antisocial was another mark against my mothering skills, according to Pete. I indulged Joey's introversion.

"Good news," Pete said.

"You're staying the night here with your guy pals?"

"No, but I will sleep in the van tomorrow night and Thursday night."

"Really? You promise?" I said.

"Yep. Your man is coming through for you." Pete reached

through the open window and patted Sophia's head. She had a fistful of my hair in her mouth.

"Your woman slept two nights in the van already and is now sleeping a third night in the van, all three of those nights with our infant," I said.

"This is the last night. Then I will relieve you of your burden." Pete leaned in and kissed me on the cheek. He told Joey to close his binder and follow him to the car.

*

That third evening in the van, a woman I recognized from the school but didn't know by name came over to the driver's side window.

"You relieving your husband for a while?" she said.

"What?" I said. "Pete's been home. He was only here for two hours so I could shower."

"Huh. I hadn't seen you. I'm Linda, by the way. Ophelia's mom." She pulled on one of her ears as though it were taffy she was stretching.

"Tia. When you'd get here?" I said.

"Monday morning. Number eight."

"Well, I've been here since eight o'clock Sunday night. Number two." I pointed to the black #2 in the van's windshield.

Linda blinked. "You keeping the baby here with you all night? Isn't it cold in there?" She glanced at the back of the van. "I wish we had space for you in the RV, but we're sharing with Shanda and Felipe."

"We're fine," I said.

"There's a bed over the cab, but you'd have to climb a ladder and with the baby—"

"We're good," I repeated.

Sophia, who had been asleep in my arms, opened her eyes. Linda waved at her.

"Well, you should come join us over by the RV. A bunch of us have been hanging out."

Of course, I'd noticed the crowd by the RV. They'd propped up the RV's awning for shade. Small children ran around the fold-out chairs where the adults drank and laughed.

"OK. Maybe I will," I said, though I knew I would not.

I watched Linda in the rearview mirror as she returned to that crowd. I noted the near-white highlights in her hair, as though a vampire had sucked the life out of those strands.

Then I did something I'd done only once before; I pulled up Pete's blog on my phone. Because I wasn't on social media, avoiding Pete's blog had been relatively easy. I'd only checked the blog out, briefly, after it took off on social media, after he developed the cult-like following. I'd read snippets of the blog post that had made him a celebrity, and then, feeling queasy, I'd quickly closed the window. Now I looked to see if he had retitled the blog. I was relieved to find that he hadn't, not yet anyhow. It was still called, only a little less stupidly, *Dad-It-Yourself.* The latest post was timestamped 6:24 p.m., only a few minutes earlier. My eyes fixated on *Some days, I'm exhausted. Some days, I don't think I'll make it through this parenthood thing. Sorry if I'm mumbling. It's been a long, hard week between work and doing all we can to get our son into the school we want him to attend for kindergarten.*

Doing all *we* can?

I pictured Joey eating cereal for dinner, alone in front of the television, while Pete wrote to his fan club. I turned off my phone.

*

When I drove to pick Joey up from school Thursday afternoon, refreshed and grateful after sleeping in my own bed for the first time in four days, I brought along a sandwich and a bottle of water for Pete. But when I pulled into the school parking lot, there were two police cars pulled alongside the road with all the campers.

Before I could find Pete to ask what was going on, one of the cops approached me and asked if I was parked alongside the street. They wanted the street cleared within fifteen minutes.

Linda from the day before swooped in after the cop to fill me in. There'd been all kinds of complaints from the neighborhood's residents. One guy had complained about headlights shining in his kid's bedroom late at night, another about honking. Others had complained about low visibility with all the cars and people. A woman told the police she was afraid she was going to run over someone's child by accident. According to Linda, the woman had insinuated that it was irresponsible to have children camping out in cars like this. Linda said, "What are we supposed to do? Call up our nannies?"

"What about kindergarten registration?" I said to Pete when I found him with the guys at the tent, which they were quickly dismantling. "I've been here since Sunday. I'm not losing my spot. I'll sit on the side of the road in a fold-out chair if I have to." I was frantic, every cell in my body buzzing.

"Don't worry. I've got it all under control," Pete said.

"You do?"

"Everybody's coming to our house."

"They're what?"

"We're moving the camp-out to our house. We have that long driveway, and there's plenty of space for people to pull off and park in our yard. It's just grass. It's just one night. Then in the morning, we'll carpool or get dropped off back at the school, and we'll line up on foot."

I looked around at all of the vehicles. Two RVs, ten SUVs, a pick-up truck, nine cars, and our borrowed van.

"The RVs alone will take up the driveway," I said.

"We'll make it work," Pete said. The way he smiled then, I could almost imagine how people could look at my husband and see someone put here to help them. I wanted to resist this feeling. I wanted to fret about the damage all these vehicles would do to our grass. But mostly I just felt relieved that Pete had figured out a way to maintain the queue, to protect the #2 slot I'd earned.

*

Getting everyone parked along our driveway and in our yard took time. Pete and Zane waved and ordered drivers about. "Pull in there." "Shift right a little more." "That's it."

Gabriel showed up with a little girl with black cat ears poking out of her brown hair. He asked if his daughter could use our restroom. He handed me an eight-pack of toilet paper. "All these people, I thought someone should contribute."

His daughter then handed me a single Gerbera daisy. "For you," she said.

I looked at Gabriel. He shrugged.

I led the girl inside the house, which was not clean by a long shot, considering not only that I hadn't been home most of the week, but also that it was near the end of the week.

As soon as the girl had closed the bathroom door, she opened it again. "I can't figure out how to lock it," she said.

"Lock's broken," I said. "I'll keep an eye on the door so that no one comes in."

She closed the door.

That's when the baby started rooting around my chest and fussing. I sat down on the sofa with her and let her nurse. I forgot all about the girl in the bathroom, until she yelled.

A woman I hadn't even known had entered my house said, "Sorry! The door wasn't locked."

The girl said, "That lady said she'd watch the door!"

I came out to the hallway with the baby suctioned to my chest, though, of course, she stopped suckling to turn her head to see what was going on, which meant my breast was now no longer even a little bit concealed.

The woman said, "Oh man, is this your house? Pete said to just walk right in. I didn't know anybody was even in here."

She'd left the front door open, the only barrier between the inside and outside a flimsy screen door with a couple of finger-sized holes in it, courtesy of Joey. Already a couple of fat flies had gotten inside. I hate flies, especially Oregon flies. They're like five times the size of Arizona flies. My introduction to those fuckers took place in a cabin on the Clackamas River. That was before I moved to Oregon with Pete, and it's a wonder I did after that trip. Those flies drove me so crazy that by the last day, there wasn't a breathing, noise-making thing inside or outside that cabin that I didn't wish dead. When the songbirds woke me before sunrise, I fantasized about them falling from the trees and landing on the lush grass in a thousand thumps. Pete said, "What kind of a monster are you?"

To the strangers in my house, I said, "We have a routine with this bathroom. We leave the door open when it's unoccupied. We shut the door when it's in use. That's how we avoid walking in on each other. Probably not going to go so well with forty-something people going in and out. I'll go get some paper and make a sign."

Now I was the sign maker.

The woman smiled nervously. "Sorry to impose on you. It's a real nice thing you and Pete are doing letting us all camp out here so we can maintain the queue. I know everyone really appreciates it."

I tried to smile back, but I wasn't confident about the shape my mouth made.

*

I cooked a frozen pizza for Joey and me. Pete had yet to come inside. All week I'd been begging him to help me and he was too busy, but now that the camp-out-for-kindergarten had become a party, he was engaged full force. He stood amongst the fold-out-chair crowd that had migrated from Linda's RV awning to our driveway. Everyone's eyes seemed to be on him, including Joey's. My son scarfed down his pizza, no doubt hoping to head back outside after dinner.

The two flies from earlier had multiplied. I counted at least seven plump bodies flying around our kitchen. I shooed them away from the pizza and Sophia's head. If I could have detonated them with my mind, I would have.

As I waved my arms and cursed, Joey said, "They're living creatures."

I ignored the comment. I was pretty certain that if Pete were the one doing the swatting, swatting flies would become a male-bonding sport.

I said, "You can take a bath in my bathroom tonight. You can sleep in my bed, too. I worry about all the bathroom traffic waking you."

Not so long ago, Joey would have grinned at the invitation to sleep in my bed. Now what he said was, "I want to sleep with Dad in the van."

I said, "Your dad's not sleeping in the van." I waved a fly away from my ear.

Joey said, "You should chill out about the flies."

Without my consciously willing it to, my hand jerked up involuntarily, then froze, hovering menacingly in midair, only this time there was no fly in my hand's path. Joey's eyes widened.

I lowered my hand, and I said, "Don't you tell me to chill out."

Joey looked down at his plate. His lip quivered.

Yes, I was disturbed that I'd almost smacked my child, but also, I felt curious. Not long ago, it had been largely acceptable behavior to smack your children when they disrespected you. I remembered my grandfather removing the leather belt, enormous steer-horn belt buckle and all, from his pants to go after my brother more than once. My own parents had sometimes threatened us with the sword-length knife sharpener that had hung next to the kitchen sink by a leather strap. I looked around at my dirty kitchen—the Cheerios crusted to the floor, the blue marker scribbles we'd yet to paint over, Joey's subpar art hanging on the walls. I looked out the window at the crowd of strangers in my driveway, my husband waving his arms like he was conducting an orchestra. I thought, what is this? Why have we assembled together to camp out all week in vehicles to get our kids into a school that is, frankly, not all that exceptional? Would our children's lives be remarkably improved by their going to this particular school? By camping out, I supposed we hoped to give our children an advantage over children whose parents couldn't take the time off work or wouldn't. But what of the children whose parents could afford to send them to private schools? I knew this: I would never know the answer. No doubt some variables could be counted on to produce clearly better outcomes than others, but I struggled to say which variables. Privilege could produce some shitty human beings. Vice versa, shitty circumstances could produce some extraordinarily kind and selfless human beings. Camping in vehicles for a week to get our kids into the best school available to them might be an act of devotion and love, but I wondered, was it rational or was it something else—some kind of mass delusion? I thought again of those wildflowers springing up from potholes. There was more than one way to look at those flowers. You could admire their tenacity, their grit. Or you could note the futility of putting down roots in a spot where you're almost certain to get trampled.

*

If Pete slept in the bed with us that night, I didn't notice him. Despite sharp parts of Joey nailing me in the lower back, the hip, the leg, I slept relatively well because Sophia slept straight through the night for the first time since we'd brought her home from the hospital.

The campers had already vacated by the time I got out of bed. I might have thought it was all a dream if it weren't for the tread marks that crosshatched our yard.

Pete had left me a note on the nightstand that he'd taken Joey to school and had what he needed to stand in line all day.

When Pete returned late that afternoon, he had registration papers in his hand.

"Your man came through for you," he said. Then he told me we had to watch the news because he was going to be on it.

My first thought was that he'd told the damn world about this Our Father thing, which meant, of course, I'd have to divorce him. No more telling myself the whole thing would blow over.

Then he said a news truck had shown up in front of the school. They'd heard about the camping out, about everyone being chased away by the police. They interviewed several people in line, and Pete was one of them.

On the news that night, a reporter talked to a bug-eyed woman who said she'd camp out for a thousand nights if that's what it took to secure her child a good education. I rolled my eyes.

When the reporter approached Pete, she said, "You've been here since Monday morning, too?"

I watched my husband say, "Since Sunday night. I was the second one here."

Gabriel, who was standing next to Pete, raised his eyebrows, and I wanted to hug him. The Pete on the news didn't notice. The Pete sitting next to me on the sofa didn't seem to notice, either. He stared intently at the television, enraptured, as did our son, who was curled up in the reclining chair with his business-card binder in his lap. In that moment, those cards made me sad in a way I had never quite registered before.

Then the reporter said, "Sleeping in a vehicle for five nights straight just to get your kid a kindergarten spot? Why is getting your kid into this school so important to you?"

Again, she held her microphone out toward Pete.

The Pete on the sofa placed his hand on my knee. I stared at that hand. Then I waited to hear what the Pete on the television would say.

SHAPESHIFTING

My mother, who doesn't know about Flynn, scrawled on a postcard a few weeks ago, "Who did this to you?" The image on the other side was of vultures ripping apart a human body face-down on a dusty road.

I responded with a postcard depicting a smiling decapitated head on a fence post: "Conceived via a bullet through the uterus. Sperm donor unknown."

In the mailbox today I find my mother's reply. It's a postcard of a child sitting before a plate of brains. Her note reads, "I've heard this one. A woman standing on a porch. A Civil War battle ensuing in the yard. A bullet rips through a Union soldier's testicle and lodges into her uterus. She gives birth to a baby boy. Son of a gun. But guns don't make women pregnant, penises do. The question is whose penis? The other question is, did you consent?"

Flynn is on the toilet as I read it to him. He gives me a look like who-talks-to-someone-about-their-mother-while-that-someone-is-on-the-toilet? When I say, "The question is whose mother, upon hearing the news of her daughter's pregnancy, asks her if she consented?!" he pulls the bathroom door shut.

I don't know why I told my mother about the embryo. I'd kept Flynn from her without a hitch. I think of those clay facial masks that purport to draw out so-called impurities: my mother the clay, the embryo the impurity.

Not that I want to be rid of the embryo exactly, but that Civil War tale feels kind of apt: that single sperm a bullet that lodged into my egg. I didn't pull that trigger. I'm an innocent bystander.

Then again, I willingly have sex with Flynn, and I don't take the pill or use a diaphragm or a condom or an IUD or a ring or whatever else is available these days. My friend Dani points this out. She says, "You knew all along this could happen. Pull-out isn't reliable birth control. I mean it can be, in theory, only you have to rely on a man to do it correctly, and therein lies the problem."

"You sound like my mother," I say.

"Only *I* don't hate men," Dani says. "I just don't want to have sex with them."

*

My mother mails me a DVD of *Rosemary's Baby* with a blue sticky note: "If you haven't seen this yet, it's time you do."

Of course, I've seen it already, but it's been a while, so I watch it again, with Flynn. He makes so much popcorn I could probably fill the bathtub and submerge all of me beneath the puffy, white blooms. He doesn't say, "You're eating for two," but the way he's been feeding me lately, I suspect he's thinking it.

"Are you worried the embryo isn't flourishing?" I ask.

"What?" Flynn says. "I just know you like popcorn."

When Rosemary wakes in the morning after being raped by Satan and she sees the scratches on her skin and asks her husband, Guy, what happened, and he says that despite her passing out last night after eating their neighbor's strange dessert, he didn't want to "miss baby night," I laugh so hard Flynn pauses the movie.

"I don't get why that's so funny," he says.

"Everything about it is funny," I say, "because everything about it is horrifying."

Flynn knows the story of my conception. When I told him, over pizza and beers when we were first dating, he became pale so quick I imagined a spile lodged in his leg, sticky blood pooling around his sneakers like sap.

Now he says, "I think your laughter is out of proportion."

"Maybe I'm laughing for two," I say.

*

At the used bookstore, where I go to find books about pregnancy and childbirth, I find a dated workbook titled *Your Parenting Self*. The scant, random questions on the perforated pages about

"Your Plans for Children" and "Making Responsible Parenting Decisions" are immediately followed by a section entitled, "Do You Know Your Own Parents?" One is encouraged to poll their parents (whom the questions assume to be a man and woman who are married) to learn the answers to an epic list of inquiries, including the following:

- If your mother/father was offered a drink at a social event, what would she/he order?
- What does your mother wear to please your father (and vice versa)?
- Does your mother/father support the ratification of ERA?
- What was a monumental disappointment in your mother's/father's life?

While Flynn cooks pasta carbonara, I say, "I already know the answers to too many of those questions. For instance, whatever drink my mother ordered, if my father was the one to bring it to her, the drink would contain a roofie. It's not hard to fill in the rest from there."

Flynn flinches. "I'm so sorry, Babe."

I say, "What does knowing your parents' disappointments and views on women's rights have to do with becoming a parent yourself anyway?"

Flynn is quiet. "I don't know," he says after a long silence.

The subject of my conception no longer drains the blood out of him, but it does drain his vocabulary, leaving little behind but "I'm so sorry" and "I don't know."

*

"*Rosemary's* Baby. Rosemary's *Baby*," I say. "I can't decide whether that wording makes the baby or Rosemary the subject of the film."

We're driving home after seeing the embryo-turned-fetus and my uterus on a monitor, both fetus and uterus black and white and grainy like television static back in the days of my youth when stations ran out of programming. Flynn said, "Holy shit! There she is!" What I said: "And *me*. That's *my* uterus."

"Definitely Rosemary," Flynn says. "It's like Rosemary's house or Rosemary's mole. The story is never about the thing. It's about the person."

"Thing?" I say.

"Figuratively," Flynn says. "In that title, the baby is Rosemary's possession. The baby has no name. The father doesn't exist."

"Says the man who didn't pull out in time."

"Pre-cum. Totally out of my control," Flynn says as he blows through a stale yellow light turning red. Then he says, "What if your mother wants to come meet her grandchild? Are you going to stash me in the linen closet?"

I assure him for the hundredth time that my mother won't visit. My mother doesn't leave the house. Ever. "But if she did, you better hope we come up with something better than the linen closet. She'd sniff you out in no time."

"I'm not afraid of your mother," Flynn says unconvincingly.

*

When I feel the fetus move for the first time, I say in a Dr. Frankensteinian voice, "It's alive!"

Flynn puts a hand to my belly, says, "Plants don't move, but nobody questions whether they're alive."

"Actually, plants do move. Just so slowly we don't register it. The point is that now I know it's not a tumor," I say. "Tumors don't kick."

Dani said the other day, "If orgasm is the little death, childbirth is the colossal death."

Now Flynn says, "You know it's not a tumor because tumors don't look like fetuses."

He returns his gaze to his tablet. I ask him what he's reading. He says an article about misogyny in the field of herpetology. Apparently, herpetology has a reputation as being a macho field. Men feeling all manly because they handle gators and snakes.

"Did I ever tell you I used to want to be a herpetologist? When I was a kid? I was really into alligators," I say.

"What does that mean—really into alligators?" he says.

"I like their ridginess, and the way they're like icebergs, showing just the tiniest bit of their bulk on the water's surface. The fetus kicking is kind of like that. A glimmer of something underneath, but what's there is still a mystery. I could be pregnant with a monster."

"Not if I'm the father," Flynn says. "No monster DNA in me, I'm pretty certain." As soon as he says it, he grimaces. Reaches across the table and rests his hand on mine. I stare at that hand, the way it makes my own hand almost disappear. I think of Flynn's Viking ancestors and his Irish clansman ancestors, all the raping and pillaging they must have cumulatively tallied up.

I pull out my hand and place it on top of Flynn's. "Don't kid yourself. There's monster DNA in all of us," I say.

*

As a kid, I used to tell other kids that my father was a monster. I was so earnest. They called me a liar. Until Dani came along, that is. She didn't roll her eyes or groan. She said, "What kind of a monster?"

I told her what my mother told me: that she didn't get a good look at him. It was dark. But she remembers he was hairy, his breath smelled like meat, he sweated a lot, and he wore a watch with a stretchy brick-like wristband that pinched her skin.

"So I'm pretty sure he's a werewolf," I said.

I liked the idea of being the spawn of a werewolf. I figured there was a good chance I'd inherit the shapeshifting gene. Shapeshifting could be useful. It didn't occur to me back then that pregnant women are shapeshifters, too. My belly is hard as a rock. I picture a huge geode, the fetus a milky quartz crystal. Shapeshifting isn't the way I'd imagined it. I'd always pictured myself behind the wheels of other bodies I assumed. This is the opposite. I'm the wheels, not the driver.

I think of my mother barred inside her parents' house, forbidden from terminating her pregnancy. Every year on Christmas morning, her mother/my grandmother spooned breakfast casserole onto a plate for baby Jesus. Never mind that even if baby Jesus were sitting at their table and could eat solid food, he wouldn't be able to fork bites of casserole; he'd need it pulverized into mush and fed to him with a tiny spoon.

My mother has said to me several times over the years, "People always tell me I laugh at inappropriate things. But I would have died a long time ago if I didn't laugh."

*

I dream I'm dissecting Flynn. I slice open his belly, peel back the skin, and pin it to our mattress.

No blood seeps out. But he's alive, watching me. He's smiling at me like I'm naked; and I realize I am naked, though not quite as naked as he is.

I expect to see his organs nestled together like pieces of a puzzle, but instead there's another barrier, his muscles. I'd forgotten about the muscles.

Although I wasn't worried about hurting him before, I am now. "Your muscles are in the way," I say.

"So remove them," he says.

I make another incision, slicing him open all over again, from sternum to navel. Then I slip my fingers inside the huge buttonhole that is his chest so I can peek inside. But there is yet another layer concealing my view, this layer composed of tiny white threads, web-like.

"What is it?" I say.

"Platelets," he says. "A clot."

"And what if I cut through that?" I say.

"Then there will be another barrier and another," he says.

I wake Flynn to tell him about the dream. "You'll never be a host, Flynn. Not unless a botfly burrows into your skin. Think about that. A creature inside your goddamned body. In your core. Directing your body's activities."

"Gut bacteria," Flynn says.

"That's a pitiful comparison," I say.

"Is it? They make neurotransmitters and hormones. Release them into our bloodstreams. Communicate with our brains," Flynn says. "Maybe your gut bacteria made you wake me ridiculously early on a Saturday to tell me how lucky I am."

*

A white envelope arrives from my mother. The larger of two stamps is of a horned dung beetle. Inside is a clickbait article my mother printed with the headline, "15 Labor Horror Stories." Attached is a yellow sticky note that reads, "Does the baby need anything?" It's signed, "Your mother."

"Tell her the baby needs a new car," Flynn says. "One with a working air conditioner and a quality stereo and one of those little convertible cup holders that can fold in to hold your sunglasses."

"That reminds me," I say. "We need an ice-cream scoop. I bent another spoon."

"Maybe what we need are better spoons."

"Maybe, but still, I want an ice-cream scoop. I've never owned a proper ice cream scoop, and I know just the kind I want. Not a perfectly round scoop shaped like a hollow hemisphere, but the kind that looks like a mouth opened wide. Like how baby birds arch their necks and open their beaks so big that from above, their mouths look like flowers. Thick, sturdy metal like it was made a hundred years ago."

"Is that what you're going to ask her for?" Flynn says.

"No," I say, "She'd send me a plastic hemisphere scoop. Also, she's not asking what *I* need. She's never asked what I need."

I'm at once both angry about this and not. Almost every feeling I have about my mother is paired with an opposite, but complementary feeling. Like the strands of DNA. Like a split end in a strand of hair, how if you pull apart the two threads, the hair unzips, and those two threads are so fragile unbonded that they break without you even trying.

*

Flynn decides to start eating paleo. To the grocery list, he adds, "meat, greens, bone broth."

Then he says, "Actually, you should try drinking bone broth, too. It's got lots of collagen. It can help prevent stretch marks supposedly."

"You're worried about my body stretching?"

"You're worried about your body stretching. I'm just trying to help."

"Did I ever tell you about my worst-ever eating experience?"

"Yes," Flynn says. "You bit into a chicken bone and chipped a tooth, and it hurt like hell, hence ruining chicken for you for life."

"And bones," I say. "I just realized that bones are ruined for me, too."

I think of my mother holed up inside her house. Her groceries delivered to her front door, everything else from QVC. The way she won't even answer the door when the mailman rings with a package in his arms. When I was a girl, my grandmother took me where the school bus couldn't: doctor's appointments, clothes shopping, choir concerts. My mother didn't try to lock me up with her, but when I left the house, she was adamant about knowing exactly where I was, always. Once when I was biking down the street to a friend's house, I got sidetracked because I found a dead snake on the road; when five minutes had passed, and I still hadn't called from my friend's phone to notify my mother of my safe arrival, she called my friend's house; and when my friend's mother said I wasn't there, my mother immediately called the police. If she would have just left the house and walked to the end of our driveway, she would have spotted me poking a stick at that dead snake.

I say to Flynn, "Fine. I'll give bone broth a shot."

Flynn reads that homemade bone broth is a thousand times better (his words) than store-bought, so he comes home from the butcher with an assortment of animal bones. "What animal is this one from?" I say, holding up a bone nearly as thick as my wrist. Flynn says, "Pig?" The randomness of the assembly makes me think of how birds sometimes line their nests with bits of human litter—scraps of paper, plastic, tin foil. I once spotted an uncoiled, but presumably unused, condom woven into a nest. Flynn simmers this hodgepodge of animal bones in a pot of hot water and herbs.

"Double, double toil and trouble; Fire burn, and cauldron bubble," I say. "I feel like this bone broth stuff is going to do something bad to me, like that strange dessert Minnie Castevet gives Rosemary in *Rosemary's Baby*."

The bone broth doesn't taste so bad. Bland mostly. Still, I know I will never drink it again. I can't stop thinking about the hardness of that chicken bone between my teeth, how the pain radiated throughout my jaw for days after. Flynn had to get a root canal a while back. He was in constant pain for weeks before that root canal. Took ibuprofen by the fistful. After the root canal he would sometimes think the pain was back, but then he'd say he wasn't sure. "How can you not be sure?" I said. "I can't tell whether it's present pain or the memory of pain," he said.

*

Three weeks before my due date, another postcard arrives from my mother, this one a photograph of a stone gargoyle with long, bony fingers and toes like fleshy talons. On the blank side, she's written, "Wishing you a happy labor!"

I've been reading books about women who indeed claim to have had happy labors. They talk about visualizing their contractions as ocean waves breaking onto sparkling, white sand. They liken their cervixes to sea anemone softly opening.

My friend Dani has a fifteen-month-old. She says, "Yeah, I read those books, too. I drank the Kool-Aid. And you know what? The Kool-Aid is the first thing you barf up when you're doubled over in pain from the contractions."

She says this between bites of lobster ravioli at a new restaurant in town.

Flynn grimaces.

Then Dani's wife Anaya says, "Worst day of my life watching her go through all that. Well, the best day, too, of course. Because, you know, the baby. But never again. I told Dani the only way we're having another one is if we adopt."

"But you have those lovely birth photos," I say.

"And my parents have lovely wedding-day photos, but they hate each other's guts," Anaya says.

I looked up images of gut microbes recently. Every image I found made me think of candy. The neon colors, the grainy textures as though the bacteria were rolled in sugar.

"Or like how my mother got me," I say. "The precious gift her rapist bestowed upon her."

Everyone is silent for a moment. Then Dani laughs so hard I know she's leaked pee. When she stops, she says, "All I have to say is thank goodness you weren't a boy."

Later, when we're sharing a subpar tiramisu, Dani says, "Did I ever tell you I used to think your mother was an honest-to-God vampire? I really did. I was both terrified of her and fascinated by her. The way she hibernated like a bat in that cave bedroom. I almost only ever saw her late at night when she was on your couch watching TV and wearing that weird purple robe that came up to her chin. She didn't even seem to see us as we walked by."

"That's because she didn't," I say.

As overly protective as my mother was when I was outside our house, when I was inside the house and she was in the vacuum of depression, she forgot my existence altogether. I learned self-sufficiency at an early age.

*

We're driving to the hospital, and Flynn says, "We never really talked about what kind of parents we want to be."

I just look at him.

Flynn says. "For instance, are we going to go to the baby when she cries at night? Or let her cry it out?"

"Go to the baby," I say. "Every time. Also, no locked doors."

Flynn starts to say something more, but my gripping the dashboard and yelling through a contraction silences him.

When the wave passes, I say, "It's simple. One rule: We ask what would my mother do? And we do the opposite."

But, of course, I know nothing is this simple.

*

My labor isn't at all like it is in any movie I've ever seen. If my water breaks, I don't see it. Maybe because I'm so out of my mind from the pain that I wouldn't know it if someone chopped off one of my limbs.

I packed a collection of six CDs in my overnight bag, but we just listen to the same one over and over and over. I wonder what Luz Casal would think if she knew she was the background music to this. When Flynn suggests putting in something else, I grip his wrist tight. "You'll mess up my rhythm," I say, even though the contractions are more like tsunamis than a gentle wave lapping at my toes. I am like a tiny crab on the sand watching that skyscraper of water darken the sky. I am worried that the only way this baby is getting out is if someone cuts it out of me.

But nobody slices me open. Nobody chops off any of my limbs. What happens is what usually happens in these circumstances, what you want to happen over any alternative scenario I can imagine: my cervix opens and out comes a human, like an escape pod abandoning ship. But she doesn't get very far before the doctor catches her and lays her on my chest. "Here's your baby," she says.

My baby? The word *baby* alone is too sentimental. The *my* is like the power of ten. I rewrite the doctor's dialogue in my head: This just came out of your vagina. Do you want it?

My insides feel like they've been ripped out, because they have been. I am gutted, but still alive. My guts are alive, too. Here they are on my chest. I try to think of the word for this. Not *undead*. But I can't think of any other word that better fits. I say all this to Flynn. I say, "What's the word I'm looking for here?"

Flynn isn't listening to me, though. The baby's fingers are wrapped around his thumb. The way he's smiling, it's like those tiny fingers are infecting him with some kind of neurotoxin. I picture microscopic tendrils uncurling from the grooves of her fingers and tapping into Flynn's.

Not that she's in control, either. None of us is in control. Not her. Not Flynn. Not me. Not my mother.

But also, we have choices. Both of these things are true at once.

PLAY IT SAFE

Jessie once drove through a hurricane because, stupidly, she'd thought the eye of the storm was far enough away that returning to her apartment in Tallahassee—she'd been staying with a friend four hours away in Atlanta—was safe. By the time she realized her mistake, it was one in the morning, and turning back with no place to stay—her two cats were in the car with her, screeching all the way—seemed even more precarious than continuing. Driving to her daughter's school carnival, where she'd have to socialize with the parents of Ellen's schoolmates in the service of raising funds for new playground equipment, felt kind of like that drive through heavy rain and wind and felled trees and the impending threat of more falling trees. She couldn't relate to these people. Take Ava's mom, for instance. Sharon was the PTA committee member in charge of organizing this carnival. The woman ended every email with "Smiles, Sharon."

Jessie puzzled over this letter closing for longer than Gabe thought warranted. "You overthink everything," he said from the passenger seat. He was drinking a vodka tonic—out of a regular drinking glass, too, not even trying to conceal that he had an open container of alcohol.

"I'm not the one driving," he said when she eyed his drink. Then he said she was just jealous and not to worry, he'd brought a flask and a small bottle of tonic water, and she could have a drink in the parking lot when they got there.

Their eight-year-old daughter, Ellen, had her headphones on in the backseat. She was watching a cartoon in which the main characters changed size and donned various techy animal suits. In a Sonoran Desert episode, one of the few episodes Jessie had watched with Ellen, the men transformed themselves into faux rattlesnakes and then observed a real, albeit cartoon, rattlesnake go after a squirrel. Cornered, the squirrel pumped extra blood to its tail and shook the tail so that in the snake's infrared heat vision, the squirrel's tail appeared to inflate like a balloon, fooling the snake into striking at the tail rather than the vital organs. Jessie had cheered when the snake missed and the squirrel escaped. Ellen had said, "Yeah, but maybe the squirrel living means the snake starves to death." That was Ellen for you. Her capacity for empathy extended even to venomous predators.

What was different about the dread Jessie felt for this particular school event versus school events of the past was that three days ago she'd been attacked while out running. She'd been running along a residential street, not a remote location, such as the trails in Saguaro National Park East, where she was always scanning the desert scrub for rattlesnakes and mountain lions. It hadn't even happened particularly early in the morning. The sun had already started to peak over the Rincon Mountains.

When she heard footfalls and turned, even though the man was dressed in jeans and was looking right at her, still her brain reasoned he must have a good reason for seeming to lunge towards her that she had simply failed to decipher. She thought he must be trying to protect her from something. A mountain lion perhaps? Though rare, mountain lion sightings did occasionally occur in town. Or maybe *he* was running from a mountain lion; he needed *her* help.

But then he crashed into her, and one hand went directly to her breast, the other over her mouth, and she understood that this man *was* the mountain lion she'd imagined.

She'd fought him off, and other than a few cuts and bruises, and the memory of his hands, she was fine really. But in her post-attack shock, adrenaline high, she'd allowed herself to be interviewed by a local reporter, who'd arrived nearly as soon as the police, and almost an hour before Gabe. He'd inadvertently left his damn cellphone in silent mode again.

The only sentence from Jessie's mouth that had not been too fouled with words inappropriate for the evening news to make the cut was "I thought hard, bony parts to soft, fleshy parts, and I rammed my elbow into his eye."

Within minutes after Jessie's face appeared on television, Sharon emailed her. "Oh my god, I just saw you on the news!

Thank goodness you're OK! Let me know if I can do anything! Smiles, Sharon."

The only reason Sharon even had Jessie's email address was because Jessie often volunteered to help out with school events, like this carnival. Parents were expected to volunteer at least twelve hours a year—not that anyone called you on it if you didn't, she knew, since Gabe volunteered at most a couple of hours. Still, if Jessie was going to attend these school events, she preferred to pass the time volunteering versus wandering around aimless. Volunteering gave her purpose, made the time pass by, so she'd signed up to "man" one of the carnival games. The wording in Sharon's email conjured for Jessie the sign outside that strip club on Speedway that read, "Earn your Man Card! Cheap Beer! Hot Babes!"

"But seriously," Jessie said to Gabe. "Weigh in here. Is she offering me smiles from her face? Or is it like a wish that I'll have something to smile about?"

"Either interpretation is friendly," Gabe said.

"You're drunk already, aren't you?" Jessie said. Then, "What are the odds that anyone there isn't going to know about this?"

"I'm proud of you. You kicked that creep's ass. You're a beast."

"What I wish is that you'd gotten there sooner so you could have reminded me I hate attention and that regular me would resent adrenaline-crazed me for fucking letting them put me on television."

She thought of her willingness to be interviewed as a fit of mad impulsiveness, the way she had once grabbed the kitchen shears and cut off four inches of hair because she'd been feeling depressed. "What are you, a toddler?" Gabe had said.

In the car, he said, "I wish I'd been there, too, so I could have killed that man."

Jessie glanced at Gabe. He was tipsy, relaxed—not at all tense the way he was years ago on the beach in La Jolla when he'd come stomping over from the surf because a guy in a yellow Speedo was talking to her.

She'd been lying on her belly, reading a horror novel, when the guy squatted inches from her face. In that yellow Speedo, the shape of the man's penis, so close she could have bitten it, had made her think of a banana.

"You have great breasts," the man had said to her, as casually as if he'd been complimenting her shoes.

Men had often commented on her breasts when she was younger. Once when she was in college, a male runner going the opposite direction had turned and yelled "Nice tits!" just after they'd passed each other on a morning run. In high school, a boy who'd been a so-called friend had nicknamed her Boobius Maximus. "Species otherwise known as Big Bouncy Breasts," he'd say in front of their other friends.

That morning in La Jolla, after Gabe had scared off the man in the yellow Speedo and she'd then told him what the man had said, Gabe had said, "Your boobs *are* nice." He'd seemed semi-pleased, as though the compliment, if you could call it that, extended to him. Then he'd said, "But I should have punched that guy."

"I hate it when you talk like that," Jessie said now as she

parked the car near the ramada where the cakewalk was always held. "Kill the man?!"

"Noted, but it's the truth. I would have probably gone psycho on that creep. Crushed his skull. Ripped his head from his neck." Gabe took another drink of his vodka tonic.

Simultaneously, Jessie felt both loved and insulted, the latter because Gabe's verbal threats concerning the man she'd physically defended herself against seemed like one-upmanship, as though he were saying he would have done better than just elbow the man in the eyeball.

*

Although Jessie was fairly certain she had never even shaken hands with Sharon, the first thing Sharon did was stand up from the ticket table and pull Jessie against her torso. She held Jessie there tentatively, as though Jessie were a dress she was trying to imagine on her body. Jessie could tell from the sad puppy-dog eyes of the other woman sitting at the ticket booth that she knew precisely what this hug was about.

When Sharon released Jessie, she studied the cut on Jessie's forehead.

"Did you need stitches?" she asked.

"Just a couple." Jessie didn't know why she said "just."

Gabe touched Jessie's shoulder. "Ellen and I will be at the jumping castle."

Jessie called out to Ellen to come give her a hug, but Ellen ignored her, ran toward the giant inflatable.

Jessie said to Sharon, "So I'm signed up for one of the games. Fishing, I think."

Sharon said, "Do you know Rick Nielsen? Noah's Dad? He's a cop. He works with that guy Dean who was on the news with you the other night."

"No," Jessie said, but she knew who Dean was. The news had cut from her to him, and he'd said, "We're proud of this young lady. She didn't let herself become a victim. And because of her smart thinking, taking a photo of the culprit's license plate, we caught him within twenty minutes of her 911 phone call."

"He was just being polite," Gabe said when Jessie said, "Young lady?!" Gabe, who was forty-seven, said, "Also, forty *is* young."

"The point is there's no way that cop is older than me. He's probably not even thirty. And he's proud of me for not letting myself become a victim? As if becoming victim of a man who wants to rape or kill you or both is a choice? Not to mention, I was knocked to the ground by that fucker. He groped my breasts. I *am* a victim!"

What burned Jessie most about the whole thing: Nothing else in life made her feel stronger than running did, yet here this guy had seen her running and thought, easy target. It was infuriating. Also humiliating—to not look half as strong as she felt. Every race she ran, she thought this time she was going to come away with a better race photo: When she saw the cameraman, she was going to straighten her posture and smile like this running thing was effortless and pleasurable. But every race photo, smile or no smile, she looked like a crumpled, snotty tissue—folded in on herself, used up.

Of course, she had managed to fight the man off, and she was impressed with herself for doing so. On the other hand, she wondered if she would have been so victorious if he'd knocked her down at, say, mile six instead of mile two. Then she might have ended up a pile of bones dug up some twenty years later.

Sharon said, "I'll introduce you when I see him."

"Why?" Jessie said.

Sharon stared at her. "I thought—" She stopped. "I guess you'll probably move your running to indoors now anyhow."

"I hate running on a treadmill," Jessie said. "I get so bored. Half the joy of running is being outside, breathing in the fresh air, taking in the scenery."

"I'd be terrified to run outside now if I were you," Sharon said.

They were standing beneath one of the pavilions at a public park where Jessie sometimes ran. The sun was setting and soon it would be dark. The children would be running around in that dark for the next two hours, parents only loosely keeping tabs on them. And this was the freaking desert. Rattlesnakes, scorpions, tarantulas—all came out at night. Yet this is where Sharon had held the carnival the last couple of years—not indoors in a gymnasium or church.

"Men harass and attack women inside and outside, whether those women are running or showering or sleeping," Jessie said. "Men brag on television about attacking women and they get elected president of the United States."

"Well," Sharon said. "But it doesn't hurt to play it safe."

Behind Sharon hung a banner that read, "Thank you for helping us raise funds to purchase new playground equipment for our children to enjoy!" Jessie pictured slides with such minuscule inclines that children had to use their arms as leverage to inch their way down; swings with five-point harnesses; monkey bars, well, monkey bars would probably be banned altogether.

Of course, no playground equipment was bully-proof, Jessie thought. No siren would sound, no electric shock would be delivered, if that kid Kyle grabbed Ellen's butt again or if Lonnie backed Ellen into a corner again and wouldn't release her until Ellen agreed that Lonnie was smarter and prettier and stronger than her.

"Play it safe" was a bullshit phrase.

Jessie said to Sharon, "I have no idea what that means." She wished now for the flask Gabe had tucked into the glove compartment of the car when she shot down his plans to carry it around in his pocket: "But the shape will show through your pocket," she'd said, thinking again of the man in the yellow Speedo years ago.

Probably, Sharon didn't think drinking while female was safe, either, like Jessie's sister-in-law, Tricia. It's not about fairness, Tricia liked to say, it's about being realistic about the risks of being too inebriated to look out for yourself. The other reason Tricia didn't drink: Because as a mother of young children, you always had to be prepared for emergencies. "What if Lexi or Kurt needs to go to the ER?" Tricia once said in earnest, "And I'm too tipsy to drive them there?" Then you dial 911, Jessie had thought. Duh.

Sharon said, "You know, like you don't run alone in the dark, for example."

Living in the desert, running in the dark was a necessity in the summers. Sure, it might be safer not to run alone, but since Jessie's runner friend, Andy, moved to Texas a few years ago, she'd yet to meet anyone else to run with. She'd said to Gabe after Andy moved, "Are you worried about me running alone at night now?" Gabe had said, "Nope. You're not in your twenties anymore. Too many other more desirable targets out there," and Jessie had playfully punched him in the arm. But in truth, Jessie appreciated that Gabe trusted and respected her enough not to treat her like a child. She appreciated that he wasn't overprotective with Ellen, either. When they went hiking up the canyon walls of Sabino Canyon, he was totally cool with Ellen walking ahead of them. Jessie was the one who had to restrain herself from making Ellen stay close, hold her hand. "What are you worried about?" Gabe would say. "That she'll fall off a cliff," Jessie would say. "Rattlesnakes," she'd say. "You know, death."

*

Each game was operated by a pair of volunteers, and the woman already sitting behind the hanging blue bed sheet—meant to represent water, Jessie supposed—was a mother of one of Ellen's classmates, Sloane. Sloane was one of the few girls in Ellen's class whose name did not rhyme with the others: Ava, Eva, Kara, Sarah. Ellen had recently, in the previous week, begun referring to Sloane as her best friend. Ellen cycled through best friends at about the rate she cycled through tubes of toothpaste, always squeezing way more than necessary and then complaining when the tubes were about a third full that it was impossible to get anything more out of them. So Jessie gave Sloane a few more weeks at best. Jessie worried a bit about what this pattern suggested about her daughter. Would she be the type of woman who falls in love easily but then finds the slightest fault or difficulty a deal-breaker?

Jessie's only interaction with Sloane's mother had been at Ellen's last birthday party, five months ago. She'd been the woman sitting alone in the back of the observation area of the gym, flipping through *Outside* magazine, while on the other side of the glass windows, the children jumped on trampolines and ran across foam-block pits. The other thing Jessie had noticed about her was how muscled her arms were. Jessie had felt self-conscious going over to introduce herself, asking the woman if she wanted any pizza. As if. The woman had politely declined, said she'd already had lunch, and Jessie had pictured a plate of plain baked chicken and roasted broccoli, no oils.

Tonight the woman's arms were concealed inside the sleeves of a hoodie, so she made a less intimidating impression.

Sharon accompanied Jessie to her game and introduced the two women. Jessie remembered the name once Sharon said it: Madge. The name conjured for Jessie the combination of "mad" and "badge," a cartoon of an angry cop.

"Game" was a misnomer for what Jessie had volunteered for. One of the women was to stand in front of the sheet and hand the waiting child a fishing pole, a long wooden stick with string hanging from the end of it, and at the end of the string, a plastic clothespin. The child was to raise the fishing pole so the string could be lowered behind the bed sheet. Behind the sheet, the second woman would clip on a treat the child would then fish out.

They agreed to take turns every half hour or so since, like Jessie, Madge had signed up for the full two hours.

If Madge knew anything about what happened to Jessie, she didn't let on. She didn't even ask about the cut on Jessie's forehead. Instead, she talked about the girls. "Sloane says she and Ellen are going to live together when they grow up. And they're going to have a dog and two cats and a rabbit. What Sloane won't tell me is where they're going to live. She says that's a secret. Ellen keeping the locale from you, too?"

"Ellen didn't tell me about it at all." Jessie was the parent who took Ellen to school, and most days, she picked her up as well, so they spent well over an hour a day chatting. In some ways, she felt like she had a good sense of what was going on in Ellen's life. And then she heard something like this and wondered what else she didn't know. Several months ago, Ellen had asked Jessie who knew her better than anyone else. When Jessie asked Ellen the same question, expecting her to name Jessie, Ellen had named Christina, the girl who'd been her best-friend-of-the-month for August.

Their first customer appeared, a boy in corduroy pants too short for his long legs. Jessie handed him the pole and started to give him instructions, but he said, "Yeah, I did this last year and the year before."

After the boy fished out the packet of peanut M&Ms Madge had clipped onto the end of the pole, he dropped the pole to the ground, ignoring Jessie's outstretched hand.

Madge said, "The teachers assure us the kids almost never need to be disciplined because they respect the learning materials and they respect the learning environment. But then outside the so-called learning environment, they throw fishing poles and leave their dirty clothes wadded between their bed and the wall. Hopefully Ellen isn't a neat freak, because if she is, Sloane is going to give her a heart attack."

Jessie said, "Ha! Ellen organizes her bookshelves by fiction and nonfiction, and within nonfiction, she organizes them by science and history and interior design. She folds her own laundry because she doesn't approve of my method. But don't worry about Ellen. She's not the fragile, OCD organizational type. She's the militant type. She'll whip Sloane into shape in no time."

Madge laughed.

But Jessie wondered. Ellen was fussy with Jessie about her things, sure, but would she really impose her will on a friend? When she'd been a baby, Ellen had put up no resistance whatsoever when other babies stole the toy with which she was playing. She hadn't even cried. She'd just looked over at Jessie as if asking, what just happened?

Gabe had long been on alert about this tendency of Ellen's to accept malfeasance so coolly. Usually, Jessie commended.

"So she's a pacifist. The world could use more pacifists." She even encouraged Ellen to empathize with kids who treated her poorly. Like when that kid Lonnie cornered Ellen in the cubby room and demanded Ellen sing her praises, Jessie had suggested Ellen consider how unhappy Lonnie must be if she's driven to bully others into making her feel good about herself. "I'm not saying you should put up with her or that you should be her friend," Jessie had said, "I'm just saying that what Lonnie did isn't about you; it's about her not feeling good about herself."

But secretly, Jessie worried Ellen, too, was an easy target, that terrible phrase.

Madge said, "I know it's November and supposedly too cool for snakes to be out, but last year on Halloween our neighbor found a rattlesnake curled up next to their front door. A trick-or-treater said, 'You have a snake by your door,' and they laughed, certain the kid was pranking them. All these kids running around in the dark, it makes me a little nervous."

Jessie had encountered ten rattlesnakes over the years. She couldn't remember what Ellen's second word was after "mama," but each rattlesnake sighting lingered in such detail in Jessie's memory she could recite the locations and the amount of light in the sky. All ten sightings had happened at around dusk. Eight of them had occurred while she was out running.

The kids' school was on a rural road, surrounded by desert cholla and prickly pear. The teachers taught the kids what to do if they saw a snake: freeze and yell, "Snake!" A snake sighting, they were taught, was justification for interrupting a teacher mid-lesson or mid-whatever. Sure enough, every year, a snake wandered onto the grounds, sometimes several. When Jessie had told Gabe's sister Tricia this, Tricia had lost her shit, acted like Jessie and Gabe were living on the Gaza Strip. "But never in thirty-something years has a child gotten bitten," Jessie pointed out. "Meanwhile, there's a school shooting somewhere in this country every couple of days."

Jessie said to Madge, "I hear you, but as my husband likes to say, you're more likely to be attacked by a rabid animal than a rattlesnake." (Sometimes Gabe substituted "creepy dude" for "rabid animal," but Jessie left this out.)

Just then, Ellen and Sloane came running toward them, slowly followed by Gabe and another man.

"We want to fish!" the girls said in tandem.

When Gabe and the other man reached them, the man put his hand out toward Jessie. "Chad Gilchrist," he said. "It's nice to meet you, Jessie. My wife's a runner. Susannah? She and her girlfriends talk about you like you're a rock star. The way you defended yourself like that?! Seriously brave."

Jessie had met Susannah when she'd helped with Ellen's class's Thanksgiving celebration the year before. Susannah had been the one who'd brought in actual nutmeg seeds and a spice grater so the children could grate fresh nutmeg for the pumpkin pie. Boy, had Ellen's teacher, Nadine, been impressed with those nutmegs. Jessie had felt like a C student with the apples, bananas, and oranges she'd brought in for the fruit salad station.

When Jessie and Susannah washed dishes in the school kitchen, Susannah had said she and her husband vet Marvel movies and Star Wars movies before they allow their kids to see them, and it wasn't just the movies they vetted, but the trailers that showed beforehand, too. "Sometimes we decide the movie is fine, but the trailers, no way; so one of us sits inside the theater and texts the other one when it's safe to bring in the kids."

Does anybody ever tell a man he's brave for defending himself? Jessie thought. And girlfriends?! Does Chad think his wife is twelve years old?

Jessie said only, "Nice to meet you, too."

Gabe said, "Throw me the car keys, Babe?"

"What for?" She squinted at him.

Gabe said, "Chad and I have a small matter to attend to in the parking lot. We'll be back in a few. Watch Ellen?"

Jessie reluctantly threw her husband the keys so he could have a faux kegger in the parking lot while she worked.

*

Sloane nuzzled up to Ellen and whispered into her ear. The way the girls looked at Jessie, Jessie wondered if Ellen had told Sloane about what happened to her.

Jessie struggled with lying to Ellen, even when it was perhaps in Ellen's best interest. Like when she spotted a dead cat in the road, Jessie would think she ought to keep her mouth shut, but instead she'd say, "Poor kitty!" and then she and Ellen would spend the rest of the drive to school mourning the cat's death and cursing the human who'd run it over.

Jessie made no exception with the guy attacking her. She didn't go into excruciating detail, of course, but nor had she told Ellen she'd just tripped on a curb.

Gabe hadn't approved of Jessie telling Ellen, but he'd backed off when Jessie insisted Ellen needed to know what kind of world she lived in.

After, both Jessie and Gabe urged Ellen to keep the story to herself. Gabe's words: "Do not tell any of your friends at school about this." Jessie's words: "Obviously, we can't control whether you tell anyone, but we think you shouldn't tell them." Ellen: "Why?" Jessie, realizing her hypocrisy as she spoke: "Because it might frighten them."

That night when Jessie put Ellen to bed, Ellen squeezed her and said, "I hope that man dies in a terrible car crash."

Breathing in Ellen's rosemary shampoo as she kissed her daughter's head again and again, Jessie had thought of all the men who had hollered at her out the windows of cars as they sped by honking, startling her. She always half-expected these men to throw an empty beer bottle. She'd pictured this in gory detail numerous times: a bottle colliding with her forehead, blood trickling into her eyes. She'd imagined the sound of tires slowing next to her, heavy footfalls pursuing her. She'd imagined running faster than she knew she was capable. She'd imagined throwing punches, doing karate kicks. She'd wondered if the stink of her very old running shorts would deter a would-be attacker. When she ran on her period, she'd wondered if an attacker would find the presence of a bloody tampon off-putting enough to call the whole thing off.

And then it happened: a man actually did attack her. And it was so wild that it was actually happening it didn't feel quite real.

Later, after the guy ran off and drove away and the police arrived, Jessie thought of a video she'd once watched of macrophages engulfing and destroying bacteria. The animation had showed a splinter lodged in a finger, allowing in the bacteria, and the narrator had said, "These bacteria are regarded as non-self substances, and the immune system will always try to destroy non-self cells." That's what it had been like when the man knocked her to the ground, like he was a splinter loaded with bacteria, and her body was on an involuntary mission to annihilate the threat.

Jessie said to the girls now, "Are you going to fish?"

"You didn't give us the pole," Sloane said, a little haughtily, Jessie thought.

Jessie held the pole out toward them, and Sloane quickly grabbed it. She broke away from Ellen and raised the pole up over the sheet.

"Wait until there's a tug on your line," Jessie said, "and then reel in your fish." She watched as Madge put her phone down and clipped not one but two packets of M&Ms onto the clothespin.

When Sloane removed her prize, she said, "One more time!"

Instead of pointing out that Sloane had already received two turns' worth of chocolate, Jessie said, "That's fine. But let Ellen have a turn first." She knew her daughter wouldn't speak up for herself in this situation, especially not when the girl cheating her out of a turn was her best friend. Ellen may be flaky when it comes to the life of her friendships, but until her passion cooled, she remained unwaveringly loyal and generous. To a fault, Jessie sometimes thought.

Sloane said, "I'll go twice, and then Ellen can go twice."

Jessie felt her body tense up. Before she could respond, Madge stood and showed her face. "Sloane, it's Ellen's turn."

Sloane squealed. "Mama! That was you?! You should have given me five packets of M&Ms!"

"I told you I'd be here the whole night," Madge said. "You seriously don't listen to a word I say."

By the time Sloane grudgingly handed the fishing pole over to Ellen, two other kids had joined the line, and once Jessie explained to Sloane that she had to go to the back of the line, Sloane was no longer interested in fishing and tugged at Ellen's sleeve. "Let's go do the darts game!"

Ellen started to hand the fishing pole off to the girl behind her, but Jessie stopped her. "But you didn't get any chocolate yet."

"It's OK," Ellen said. "I want to play darts with Sloane."

Jessie studied Sloane. She was a tall, thin girl—half a foot taller than Ellen. In those green leggings and fitted long-sleeve T-shirt, she looked like a praying mantis. The way Sloane's panties, clearly visible beneath her leggings, bunched up reminded Jessie of the veiny flesh of a cabbage. Though all the girls' panties showed beneath their leggings, too—what was the alternative, little girls' thongs?—Sloane's panty lines, because she was so tall, seemed inappropriate somehow, less innocent. Jessie was wrong for thinking this, of course. Sloane was eight as well, a child. Jessie was allowing her anger at Sloane for treating Ellen poorly affect how she saw the girl's body. She was projecting her anger onto Sloane's body. Isn't that what creep monster men did? Isn't that what her attacker had done? Projected his anger or resentment or whatever onto Jessie's physical body?

The next girl in line complained. "This is taking forever."

"Take your turn, Ellen," Jessie said.

Ellen looked to Sloane, then back to Jessie.

Jessie remembered how when she was pregnant with Ellen, she'd said to Gabe that she hoped more than anything else that their baby would grow up to be kind. Gabe had screwed up his face at first, but then agreed she had a point. Of course, she'd not meant kind to the point of making an easy victim. Maybe that had been the worst thing, more so than being seen by her attacker as an easy target: the excruciating miscalculation Jessie had made, how she'd so foolishly believed that man was there to help her. Perhaps it was testament to Ellen's self-preservation that she cycled through best friends so frequently. People sucked.

Still, how much of an asshole did Sloane have to be before Ellen finally stuck up for herself?

Gently, encouragingly, Jessie said, "Two minutes ago, you were excited to fish. Fish, Ellen. It's your turn."

Jessie could feel Madge, Sloane, and the other kids all watching them.

"Mom," Ellen whispered, embarrassed.

Then Madge said, "Ellen, catch!" and she tossed a packet of M&Ms toward Jessie's daughter. The packet pelted Ellen in the shoulder and fell to the ground, and with it, so did Jessie's heart.

"Oops! So sorry, Ellen!" Madge said.

Jessie watched anxiously as Ellen bent over to pick up the projectile that had struck her, taking small comfort in knowing Ellen hadn't really been harmed.

THE SAND
AND THE SEA

On our way home from the beach, my mother parks the car in the gravel parking lot of an ice cream shop. When she returns with three Band-Aid-colored cones topped with mint chocolate chip, my sister is hanging halfway out her window to intercept her treat. I accept one of the cones, but I don't thank my mother, and she doesn't demand I do. We eat the ice cream in the car, my skin stinging where dozens of jellyfish tentacles caressed my limbs as I swam back to shore from what seemed like a mile out. The current carried me away on the little pea-green raft I won in a coloring contest. I had to ditch my prize to break free of the current's pull. My mother doesn't say she's sorry I almost drifted out to sea. She doesn't say she's sorry she wasn't watching me. Or that it's time she learns how to swim. She says, "Good chocolate chip to ice cream ratio in this."

*

When my mother returns from the grocery store, my sister's friends from the neighborhood hover like seagulls as we help my mother unload the trunk full of heavy bundles, each double-bagged. In the kitchen, my mother unveils her purchases like a returned traveler showing her souvenirs. "These were on clearance." "This I've never seen before, but the cashier said they're delicious." When she empties plastic bags of miniature chocolate bars into the silver candy bowl, my sister sifts the candy between her fingers like the seashells she brings home in a red pail every trip to the beach. Her friends stare at the bowl. When my mother says, "Help yourselves," I watch from the doorway as they swoop.

*

"My childhood was terrible. You can't imagine how terrible," my mother says. Although I know from my father that my mother has four siblings and that her parents are still married and living in the same house she grew up in, always I imagine just my mother and her mother, nobody else. They live by the sea in a house made of candy my mother isn't allowed to eat. Her mother warns that removing just one peppermint or gumdrop could bring the whole house down and that if the house falls, they'll be ravaged by the sea.

*

The morning I am almost dragged out to sea, a woman hauls crabs up out of the ocean in a wire cage, minutes after I beach. The crabs don't move inside the wire box behind her, as though they are content being caught or, otherwise, already dead, though I know they're not. Always, my mother drops them into the boiling water alive.

*

Years later, my mother returns the little blue reply card to say she won't be able to attend my wedding. It's accompanied by a heavy package, like those she sent me when I was in college, despite how many times I explained that the distance between the school post office and my dorm room was nearly a mile and that I had to carry those packages on foot. In contrast to the sticky baklava and tins of chocolate covered pretzels in the college packages, this package contains a set of serving bowls painted with brown and blue nautilus shells.

*

I spend the night on a beach in Bolivar with a girlfriend and a couple of boys we meet on the Galveston Strand. When I enter the back door in the morning, sand sticking to my legs, my mother is in the kitchen, but she doesn't look at me, doesn't ask where I've been. She says to my husband, the one time she meets him, "She was always an independent kid. She never needed me."

*

The woman with the crabs stops and stares at me and at my mother in her jean shorts and faded red T-shirt. My mother doesn't own a swimsuit. The woman says, "This beach is no place for kids with a mother who doesn't know how to swim. You should take those girls down to the lifeguarded beaches." Through the woman's blue cover-up, I can see the softness of her breasts and belly and hips.

*

I've never seen my mother naked. This strikes me as odd now that I'm a mother. My kid sees me naked all the time. She brushes her teeth in my bathroom. She begs to take bubble baths together. She reaches up underneath the sleeves of my shirts to rub my arms as though with enough effort, a genie will emerge from my fingertips.

*

I wonder: if I could travel back in time and mother my mother, would everything have turned out different? If someone would have hugged her and tenderly brushed her hair and said to her, "I would swim across the ocean for you."

*

When I emerge from the ocean that morning, I lie limp and heavy on the sand like a wet towel. When I look up from my mother's white sneakers and fuzzy peach ankle socks, I see she is frightened. What she says is, "I'll pour salt water on you to take some of the sting out." She borrows my sister's red pail and runs back and forth between me and the sea. Like a child determined to fill a moat around a sandcastle, only to find upon each new return that the sand's appetite is greater than she thought possible.

WHAT DOESN'T KILL YOU

As Annabelle rode the escalator down to baggage claim, a woman a few steps ahead lost her footing and tumbled down the toothed metal stairs like an unwieldy duffel bag down a luggage chute. When the woman struck bottom, Annabelle considered the hidden damage that may have occurred: bones snapped like willow sticks, soft organs bruised like dropped fruits. Although Annabelle always swaddled breakable items carefully in the folds of her clothes when she traveled, once she'd had to shake the entire contents of a suitcase to remove tiny shards of glass-like sand from a beach towel.

Two men lifted the woman to her feet and helped her to a black cushioned seat. She looked more embarrassed than anything else. She was young, in her late twenties maybe. Someone brought her a bottle of water from a vending machine, and she spilled it on her polka-dotted blouse as she drank.

Annabelle considered telling the woman she shouldn't feel embarrassed. These things happened. And they had little to do with you. Falling down an escalator wasn't even bad in the scheme of things. No one else was harmed, after all.

Babies drowned in bathtubs when their parents ran to answer the telephone. People's grown children armed themselves, went out into the world and fired guns at crowds of strangers. The unofficial reason Annabelle was in Tucson, in fact, was to visit the Safeway where a little over a month earlier a man had killed six people and severely injured that congresswoman.

Annabelle's friend Paula had visited her daughter in New York City a few days before 9/11. Though Paula hadn't been in the city when the towers collapsed, you wouldn't know it the way she went on about how she could have been one of those people inside. Above Paula's mantle sat a framed photograph of the towers. She ordered it after. You'd think the towers were relatives of hers, a pair of aunts who'd taught her how to play gin rummy.

This time around, Annabelle would be the one with the story to tell. Already she was who everyone was talking to. All her friends had called to ask was Dennis and his family all right? Did they live close to that Safeway? Had they known any of those people?

Paula, too. She'd sent Annabelle a card. *What a dreadful tragedy! I'm so relieved to hear that Dennis and Jayde and Lela are OK. I'm keeping them and their neighbors in my prayers.* The card was printed with cherry blossoms, and Annabelle saved it between pages in her Bible study book.

Annabelle's official errand in Tucson was to watch her granddaughter Lela for a few days so Dennis and Jayde could drive up to Phoenix for a weekend alone. Marriage trouble.

Annabelle had known there'd be trouble the first time she met Jayde. They'd gone on a whale sightseeing tour just outside the San Diego Bay, and while everyone else marveled over the dozens of bottlenose dolphins skipping along the water near the ship's hull, Jayde talked about how male dolphins gang rape the females and then murder the resulting offspring.

When Dennis called to ask her to come out to Tucson for a long weekend, he said he hated asking her at the last minute, but "we're in need of some routine maintenance." Then he said, "But don't tell Jayde I said that."

And therein lay the real problem with Dennis's marriage. He'd married the sort of woman who might scold him simply for talking to his mother.

Other than the fact that they both loved Dennis and Lela, Annabelle seemed to have nothing in common with her daughter-in-law.

Jayde was a fitness trainer, paid to help people exercise. Once, Dennis had taken Annabelle to the gym to pick Jayde up because her car was in the shop, and Annabelle had watched through the long glass window as Jayde supported the muscled arms of a man lifting a barbell that looked heavy enough to crumple the roof of a car. Annabelle hadn't been able to look Dennis or Jayde in the eye that evening.

Soon after that, she'd had a dream that Dennis, Jayde, and Lela had come to Ohio to visit, but Jayde was so tall she'd had to get down on her hands and knees and crawl through the front door of Annabelle's house. Annabelle had been ashamed in the dream—for being so small, for Dennis being so small, for her house being so small, even though in real life, Annabelle was actually a couple inches taller than Jayde, five and a half feet to Jayde's five feet four, and her house was at least twice the size of Dennis's and Jayde's house.

*

Lela ran out of the house to greet Annabelle when she pulled into the driveway in her rental car. Lela threw her arms around Annabelle, and Annabelle said, "I want to stuff you into my suitcase and smuggle you home with me."

Lela looked as though she'd witnessed a hummingbird crash into a window.

Annabelle said, "I miss you is what I'm saying. You're my girl."

Lela said, "I'm my own girl."

Annabelle said, "Yes, but you're my girl, too."

Other than her full lips, Lela didn't much resemble her mother. One could have said the same about Annabelle and Dennis, only nobody ever had because they at least shared the same skin color. Jayde, on the other hand, complained about how strangers gave her sideways glances as though they thought she'd kidnapped Lela. They asked if she'd adopted her.

Lela said, "Did you get me anything?"

Years ago, Annabelle wouldn't have expected to be in the position to lavish her grandbabies (current count: one) with much of anything but cheap candy, so it was with great pleasure that she presented Lela with one of the little robot bugs that Lela collected. This one was chunky like a cockroach. All Annabelle remembered Dennis playing with as a kid were baseball cards.

Soon, Jayde helped Annabelle with the luggage, and then Annabelle sat at the dining table while Jayde washed dishes. Annabelle offered to wash them for her, but Jayde refused.

Lela disappeared into her bedroom. If Jayde hadn't been there, Annabelle would have followed her. She saw Lela so infrequently that she gladly did whatever Lela wanted when they were together. Her last visit, she'd permitted her grandchild to paint both their nails a metallic gray from Jayde's stash. Their fingers looked bruised afterwards, as though they'd slammed every one of them in the jamb of a door.

Annabelle pulled at her blouse to air herself out. February, and it was over eighty degrees already. The desert sun was like an antacid fizzing into the landscape, permeating everything.

She said, "So, a weekend alone, just the two of you? That'll be nice."

She noted the kitchen floor mat's frayed ends and the dirt stains and the way its dull red clashed with the orange polish on Jayde's toes. She added *buy new kitchen floor mat* to the list in her head of tasks that needed doing before she took a plane back to Ohio.

Jayde said, "I'm running a marathon. Dennis didn't tell you why we asked you to come out?"

Annabelle was pretty certain she knew why Dennis hadn't mentioned the marathon. Because it was beside the point.

"But you're not taking Lela, so that will give you two time alone together."

"Sure. But mostly it's that I have to get to bed early the night before the race. She's been having nightmares from time to time. Nothing major, but some nights she wakes up crying, and it takes some effort to get her back to sleep." All this she said with her back to Annabelle while she sloshed plates and silverware around in soapy water.

"Nightmares! That poor baby," Annabelle said.

Jayde shrugged. "Didn't Dennis and Cole have nightmares when they were little?"

"Not that I'm aware of," Annabelle said, but that wasn't exactly true. Her boys had occasionally cried in their sleep, and every time, she'd felt sick with guilt.

Although she and Jayde had never talked about it, Annabelle knew Dennis must have told Jayde about the years she'd spent married to her second husband, Randy, after Dennis's and Cole's father left. It embarrassed her that Jayde knew about that.

Annabelle asked about the nightmares, what they were about.

Jayde said she had no idea. She shuffled items around in the pantry. She liked to be busy, or at least she did whenever Annabelle was around. From the state of the house—bits of what looked like fried egg on the floor, handprints on the windows—Annabelle could see she wasn't so busy all the time.

Then Jayde said, "If she were to wake up crying in the hotel room the night before the race, *that* would be a nightmare."

"How many miles is this race?"

"It's a marathon. All marathons are 26.2 miles." She sounded annoyed, but Jayde ran all kinds of races; Annabelle couldn't possibly be expected to keep all these distances straight.

"How long do you expect it to take you? A couple of hours?"

"What do you think I am? An Olympic athlete?! Try three and a half hours."

"I can't imagine," Annabelle said, "running like that for fun."

"I never said it was fun. I mean it is part of the time," Jayde said. Then, "Like they say, what doesn't kill you."

Annabelle had read that it was because the bullet passed through only one lobe of the congresswoman's brain that she survived. In the article, a doctor compared the human brain to a twin-engine plane. Lose both engines, and you're a goner. Lose just one engine, and you may be able to putter on.

She said, "I'd like to see that Safeway while I'm here. Is it close?"

Jayde pulled her head out of the pantry and stared at Annabelle. "What are you talking about?"

"I want to see where that shooting happened."

"Why on earth would you want to do that?"

"Did you hear she recently asked for toast for breakfast? A bullet to the brain. It just goes to show you."

"Show you what?"

"What people can survive, what they can overcome. With God's help, of course."

"Six of those people didn't overcome."

"Makes her recovery all the more miraculous," Annabelle said.

Unlike her friend Paula, who liked to imagine she'd come close to danger, Annabelle knew danger firsthand. She'd jumped, and with two kids, no less; and God had saved all three of them, placed them gently onto safe ground. He'd rescued them from a lifetime of worrying that Randy was going to find them and kill them.

Jayde shook her head. "What it shows me is sometimes bullets miss their marks."

*

When Dennis came home from work, they ordered Chinese food. Annabelle and Lela shared a Styrofoam box of chicken chow mein. Dennis and Jayde drank wine with their food, as usual.

Lela held up her chocolate milk, declared that it was wine, and said, "A toast to Grammy!"

Annabelle reached across the table to clink her glass of iced tea with Lela's milk. She awkwardly tapped Dennis's and Jayde's glasses on her way back.

Annabelle said, "Let's see, did I tell you Cline and his brother are going to Greece next month? For three weeks. I wish you and Cole got to see each other more often."

Dennis said nothing of Cole. Instead, he said, "Why aren't you going?"

"Oh, Cline's brother's wife isn't going, either. I'm really busy with my volunteer work at the church, and Cline and I travel plenty together. To tell you the truth, it'll be kind of nice to have him out of the house for a little while." She laughed.

Jayde and Dennis gave each other a quick look.

"Well, good for them," Dennis said. "Good for them."

Annabelle couldn't stop herself then. She reached out and put her hand on Dennis's. "I'm so sorry we never went anywhere, that we never had anything. I'm so sorry for all of it."

"You don't owe me any apologies," Dennis said.

Unlike Cole, who said things like, *Mom, I love you, but to be honest, I don't know that I'll ever really move past that time*, Dennis never wanted to talk about those years. Even when he was a boy, Dennis had been a mystery. The apartment she and the boys lived in after they fled Randy had had a washing machine with half the control panel ripped off, the circuit board exposed. She set the dial and then pressed this one particular metal node with the blunt end of a plastic butter knife to start the machine. She knew that much because the landlord had shown her. But she hadn't understood the first thing about how or why the machine started when she pressed that node or what would happen if she messed with any of the other exposed parts, and so it was with Dennis.

She wondered, however, if he was settling up with her, too, only in a less obvious manner than Cole, who always had his hand out. This last-minute request for her to come to Tucson, for instance.

"You didn't have anything?" Lela asked.

"I just mean we couldn't do things like go on vacations or go out to restaurants, stuff like that," Annabelle said.

"You didn't have food?"

"We had food. We ate what was in the house is all."

"What she means is we ate Spam," Dennis said. He laughed loudly.

"What's Spam?" Lela asked.

"It's meat in a can," Dennis said.

"I didn't have much money back then, Lela," Annabelle said.

Jayde led Lela to the bathroom to bathe her.

Annabelle said to Dennis, "I'll write you a check for the hotel this weekend. My treat."

Dennis said, "You've done enough, Mom. We really appreciate you flying out like this."

He took Lela's plate to the sink.

"Here, let me clean up." She took the plate from him, but he continued to clear off the table. Keeping busy, just like Jayde.

She said, "Jayde said she's running a race this weekend."

"Did I not tell you that?"

Annabelle wanted to say that he didn't need to lie, that she could care less that their weekend alone was also a race weekend. But what she said was, "Will you give me directions to that Safeway?"

"What? Jesus."

She ignored his word choice. "It's a national story. Everybody's talking about it. Why shouldn't I want to see it while I'm here?"

When she'd called him a month or so earlier, he'd said yes, they were fine, and no, the store wasn't close by, and no, they didn't know any of the victims. Then he said he didn't want to talk about it anymore.

Now he said, "It's not a tourist site."

*

It was nearly seven when Dennis and Jayde pulled out of the driveway. Jayde rolled down the window to say to them, "Only one book. It's late."

Back in the house, Annabelle said to Lela, "Did your parents say they're just going to Phoenix this weekend for a race?"

"Maybe they're going there to die," Lela said nonchalantly.

"Oh! Why would you say something like that?"

"Everyone dies. I'm going to die. You're going to die. Grandpa's going to die. Uncle Cole—"

"OK, I get the point."

There was something to admire in Lela's unabashed acceptance of this simple fact of life. Her earnestness reminded Annabelle of Dennis when he'd been a kid. But she suspected something else lurked behind that insouciance. Her grandbaby had been having nightmares, after all.

"Let's go get you ready for bed, Pickle."

Annabelle sat on the toilet lid and brushed Lela's teeth. She skipped the flossing. It was near impossible to see into that little mouth and putting her fingers in there was awkward and dirty, quite frankly.

Lela cited the break in protocol.

"I'm sure it's not a big deal if we skip one night."

"Did Mama say it's OK?" She looked skeptical.

"We don't have to tell her, do we?"

Lela grinned. She ran and threw herself onto her bed, which was the same size mattress Annabelle had shared with Dennis and Cole after they fled Randy.

When Annabelle showed Lela the Bible story books she'd brought for her, Lela said again, "Did Mama say it's OK?"

Annabelle said, "These are the same stories I read your daddy when he was a kid."

Lela rested her head against Annabelle's shoulder while Annabelle read, and several times Annabelle had to shift because her granddaughter's skull pressed too hard into her shoulder bone or clipped her chin. Like cuddling with a hammer.

After, Lela said, "I don't ever want to be swallowed by a whale."

Annabelle said, "I heard you've been having nightmares. Want to tell me about them?"

"Once I dreamed I didn't have a seatbelt on, and there was no top on the car, and we crashed, and I flew out of the top and landed on the road. Then a motorcycle drove over me."

Annabelle said to Lela, "How about we pray to God to keep us safe?"

"God's the one who put Jonah in the whale."

Annabelle said, "While being in the whale was scary, really the whale saved Jonah from drowning. It turned out to be a good thing that whale swallowed Jonah."

Lela looked dissatisfied. "It would have been better if God had just saved Jonah from drowning without making him have to be swallowed by a whale."

On that whale sightseeing tour where she first met Jayde, Annabelle hadn't seen any whales, only a whale spout from a great distance. Like finding a scrap of a shed snakeskin on your porch. But later, on another tour, she'd seen a blue whale, the largest animal that had ever lived on Earth. Its long, torpedo-shaped body shimmered like an opal as it passed below the water's surface a few meters from the ship. The animal was huge, yet it was there and then gone so fast Annabelle felt afterwards as though she'd imagined it. Like the ocean blinked open a great eye and then quickly closed it again.

Annabelle kissed Lela's hair. "Sometimes God tests us. To help us become stronger." Then, "Would you like me to sleep with you tonight?" Although Jayde had said she'd put fresh sheets on their bed for her, Annabelle didn't want to sleep in Dennis's and Jayde's bed.

But Lela said, "No, thank you."

Annabelle stood there, stunned.

The last time Lela had visited in Ohio, she'd slept between Annabelle and Cline three nights straight.

Now Lela yawned and pulled the sheet up over her eyes. "Could you turn the light out?"

*

After a breakfast of banana pancakes in the shape of Mickey Mouse, Annabelle took Lela to Agua Caliente Park about a mile from the house to feed the turtles. Before they left the house, Lela said her mother said it was illegal to feed the turtles, that it was bad for the turtles, too.

Annabelle said, "I distinctly remember that the sign says not to feed the ducks. It says nothing about turtles."

Soon, they sat on a metal bench shaded by bearded palm trees with elephantine trunks and threw corn puffs into the pond and watched the turtles' heads poke up to swallow the soggy cereal.

The ducks were occupied with the breadcrumbs a group of children a little ways down tossed to them. "Duck! Duck!" the children said. Annabelle was glad to be able to feed the turtles without the ruckus of ducks flapping their wings and nearly clobbering the poor turtles as they surfaced.

At first count, there were six turtles, but in no time at all, there were too many to count, what with the way they dove down and disappeared into the murky water before reappearing in another location.

"There's like a million billion of them," Lela said.

"My goodness, just look at all those turtles!" a woman said from behind them. A bulldog sat next to her. She had it tethered by a studded leash.

A man approached on a wooden cane and said there used to be even more turtles when the water line was higher. "Once I saw a blue egret in the reeds," he said.

"Get your bone, Jackie!" the woman said to the bulldog. "Get your bone, you dummy, you fool. If I had that bone, I'd be like, that's my bone!"

The man said, "Almost all the water's dried up now."

A couple of teenage boys jumped across a thin stretch of water onto a tiny island about the size of Dennis's and Jayde's kitchen. They wore black T-shirts and backwards baseball caps. Their skin was pasty. The most distinguishing difference between them was one was chubby, the other lanky. The lanky boy reached into the water alongside some reeds and came out with a small turtle that frantically wiggled its legs. Both boys laughed.

"Look," the other boy said. "It's trying to swim away!"

Lela stared at the boys. "Are they hurting that turtle?"

Annabelle said she didn't think so, but she watched them, too.

The boy put the turtle down onto the dirt, and the animal scrambled back towards the water, but just before it escaped, the boy grabbed it again.

"They picked that poor animal up," the woman with the bulldog said.

The man with the cane said, "It's illegal to handle the turtles. It's illegal to feed them, too." He stared at the bag of corn puffs in Lela's hands.

"I told you," Lela said.

"The sign doesn't say *not* to feed the turtles," Annabelle said.

"Trust me. It's illegal," the man said.

"Somebody ought to do something about that turtle," the woman with the dog said. "That boy's going to hurt that turtle."

"What can anyone do?" Annabelle said.

The boy held the turtle up so he could look at its belly. The other boy wiggled a stick at it.

Lela said, "You could tell them to leave it alone."

"Honey, those boys aren't going to listen to me," Annabelle said.

"It's illegal," the man said again.

"You going to write them a ticket?" Annabelle said.

The man walked away, and soon Annabelle and Lela did, too.

In the car, Lela stared at the floorboard.

Annabelle said, "They'd just catch another one as soon as we leave."

Lela said, "Why won't God just save the turtle now because it's the right thing to do?"

Annabelle pictured the turtle rising from the boys' hands and levitating there in the air above them, just out of their grasp, like something you'd see in a superhero movie. The invisible hand of God.

When the boys were little, she'd made up a superhero while washing their sleek boy bodies in mounds of bubbles. Bubble Woman had three superpowers: (1) she could blow bubbles into the eyes of foes, (2) she could morph into lathery water and slip through pipes and crevices to make a quick escape, and (3) she could fill a room with bubbles in a matter of seconds so her enemies couldn't see what was in front of them. Bubble Woman would have also had the power to seal herself inside an impenetrable bubble, except Dennis had complained that if she could do that, then she'd sit safely inside a bubble all her life. There would be no story.

Annabelle's friend, Paula, mused that God saved that congresswoman by deflecting the bullet as it entered her skull so that it just missed killing her. But Annabelle wondered if maybe he saved her by allowing the bullet to enter her skull in the first place.

For three years, Annabelle had prayed to God to take Randy away by whatever means necessary. When she'd left Randy, she'd felt as though she were abandoning God, too.

Then, after she'd driven the boys across the country and they'd gotten set up in an apartment of their own, and after she'd spent about two weeks jerking her head at every little sound and peeking through the blinds a couple dozen times a night, and after she'd more or less accepted that she'd signed on to a lifetime of this restless vigilance, one night she saw a flash of electric blue light streak across the sky. A meteor, probably. Whatever it was, it felt like a wink to say, *I see you.*

A few months later, Randy was dead. Drove his truck into a median at eighty miles an hour. Fell asleep at the wheel, maybe, the police said.

If Annabelle had gained something from her experience with Randy, she didn't know what it was. But her not being able to see it didn't mean nothing was there.

*

They were in the shallow end of the heated public pool for barely ten minutes when every lifeguard on deck blew their whistles and commanded the swimmers to get out. Annabelle had been sitting cross-legged so that the water came up to her neck, the pool like a great amoeba ingesting her. Lela had splashed around her, pretending to be a shark eating a fish and then a lion eating a mouse. Then, she'd pretended to be a turtle being pulled out of the water by a mean boy. "Put me back! Put me back!" Lela had said as she wriggled her arms and torso as if she were having an epileptic seizure. It was not Lela's fake seizure the lifeguards were responding to, but the prostrate body of a boy on the cement alongside the pool's deep end.

Annabelle and Lela joined the other swimmers in the grassy area alongside the outer perimeter of the pool. They sat on towels and watched as the teenage lifeguards made a circle around the boy, and another lifeguard kneeled by the boy. The lifeguards looked about helplessly as though they had not been trained to handle incidents that occurred outside the water.

A couple of girls slightly older than Lela sat nearby. The one in the red bikini and with waist-length hair said, "I had to go to the hospital once to have a penny taken out of my throat."

The other girl, who wore a rainbow-striped bikini and sported a pixie cut, said, "I think he's dead."

"No one died yet," the first girl said.

The lifeguards spread out their towels and held them up between them, effectively shielding the boy's body from the crowd's view. Annabelle suspected they did it more to conceal their own ill-preparedness than to shade the boy from the sun.

When the ambulance appeared, the first girl said, "They're going to take him to the hospital. His family is going to follow in their car."

The second girl said, "Oh my god, they're going to shock him! I can't watch." She didn't cover her eyes, though.

"He came to! He came to!" the first girl said.

"I bet he was running," the second girl said.

"Totally," the first girl said. "That's why you're not supposed to run around the pool."

Annabelle spoke up then. "You're right that it's not safe to run around a pool, but I wouldn't say that's why he slipped. He could have slipped walking, too, I bet."

The girls stared at Annabelle.

Then Lela said, "But it's easier to slip if you run."

Annabelle started to say something, but then they all turned to watch the boy wheeled into the back of the ambulance. The lifeguards gave the signal that it was OK for everyone to return to the pool. They hollered, "Walk, don't run!"

The three girls grinned at Annabelle.

Then they turned and ran anyhow, even Lela. Their thin legs scissored the air. They hurled their bodies into the water, screamed as they fell.

*

That evening, a few minutes after Lela called Dennis and Jayde to video chat, she came running into the kitchen to say her mother wanted to talk to Annabelle.

On the computer monitor, Jayde said, "Lela says she had a nightmare last night about being swallowed by a whale."

Annabelle felt as though Jayde had launched a dish at her. "What?"

All day, she'd been with Lela, and Lela had not said a word about the dream.

Jayde said, "I'd prefer you didn't read her those stories."

Annabelle said, "You said yourself she's been having nightmares."

Jayde raised her eyebrows the way she did sometimes.

Where was Dennis? Why wasn't he here to defend her?

Outside, an ice-cream truck drove by, and Annabelle wished Lela would hear it and come running. She would lift that baby into her arms and run after the ice-cream truck as fast as she could to get the driver's attention, no matter how her bare feet might blister or her breasts jiggle, no matter that she had a rule against buying ice cream from a truck on account of a lot of those guys being child molesters or drug dealers, not to mention the ice cream was overpriced.

Jayde said, "Think about it. The man is punished because he doesn't do what God tells him to do. It's a story that teaches her to be afraid, to obey."

"Oh, I don't think so," Annabelle said.

After Lela and the other girls had crashed through the water and then rose back up to the surface, a lifeguard had been standing at the edge of the pool waiting for them. He'd said that if they ran again, they'd be asked to leave. The girls had nodded, then burst into giggles as soon as the lifeguard walked away.

"Well, I do," Jayde said. "A lot of those stories are like that. Abraham. Job."

On the way home from the pool, Lela had told Annabelle about being in the car with her mother and being pulled over by the police. She'd said Jayde had seemed scared. Annabelle struggled to imagine it. When she'd asked Lela what the officer pulled her mother over for, Lela had said, "Driving while Black." Annabelle changed the subject after that.

When Dennis finally appeared, he said only, "We have to go to dinner. We have a reservation in ten minutes." He acted as though he didn't notice her staring at him, a dirty sponge in her hand.

*

Annabelle scrubbed and scrubbed the inside of the teapot with a piece of steel wool, scratching away years' worth of calcium deposits. When the teapot shone again, she said to Lela, "Why didn't you tell me you had a nightmare last night?"

Lela looked at the tile floor.

Dennis and Cole never told her about their childhood nightmares, either, as far as she could recall. Perhaps because they'd known she would have cried. She was always crying back then.

"Just tell me why," Annabelle said. "Why didn't you tell me?"

"Because you read me that book. It's your fault." Lela raised her eyes.

Annabelle said nothing for a long moment. Then she told Lela to put on her shoes. They were going out.

"My jammies won't be clean," Lela said as they pulled out of the driveway.

"Are you planning to lie on the floor?"

"No."

"Are you planning to roll around on the deli counter?"

"No."

"Then your jammies will stay clean."

"They won't."

"I'll get you an ice cream. I'll get you anything you want."

Lela shut her mouth.

Along the drive, Annabelle had to hit the brakes to avoid a bicyclist who crossed over the white line into her lane. She honked. The guy gave her the finger. Annabelle honked again.

"Did you almost hit him?" Lela said.

"He swerved into my lane."

He was lucky she hadn't hit him. It wouldn't have been her fault if she had.

They pulled into the parking lot of the Safeway, which had big arches to walk through on the way in, similar to the arches at the entrance to Annabelle's church. Behind the building, the Santa Catalina Mountains loomed large, the weathered spine of something ancient.

A memorial took up an entire set of windows. There were the congresswoman's campaign posters; red, white, and blue bows larger than human heads; and bouquet after bouquet of flowers.

Lela complained she was cold. Annabelle had forgotten to grab Lela's jacket, forgotten that the temperature in Tucson could drop twenty degrees or more at sunset.

"We'll just have to walk faster. It'll be warmer in the store." But, of course, the Safeway would not be warmer.

"Just look at all those flowers," Annabelle said. She fished her disposable camera out of her purse and snapped a few pictures.

Inside, the Safeway looked like any other Safeway. It was lit up like a theme park after dark. A huge red circle was high up on the back wall; a subtle swivel of an "S" ribboned through it. The irony of the store's name was not lost on Annabelle. Not that you could blame Safeway. You couldn't blame anyone other than the guy who'd done it and maybe not even him. They said he was crazy. Blaming a mentally unsound person for their actions was like blaming the ocean for producing a tsunami. There wasn't much sense in it.

On the other hand, she supposed the parents were partly responsible. There was no getting around responsibility for the people your kids became, for you were the one who sent them to school without getting every last nit out of their heads, and who borrowed money out of their piggy banks, always intending to repay them with interest the second you could.

Still, in the end, tragedies happened no matter what kind of decisions you made. You lost your footing on an escalator. A crazy man pointed a gun at you. There was comfort in knowing this.

Annabelle told Lela there was something they needed to do before they got the ice cream. She took her up to the customer service desk, and when the young man with a grain of rice in his beard asked Annabelle how he could help her, she said, "I was wondering if you could tell me where exactly in the store it happened."

He blinked at her. "I'm not authorized to talk about that."

"All I want to know is where."

He looked down at Lela in her jammies, then back up at Annabelle. "I'm afraid I can't help you."

"You could show me with your eyes. Just a quick look of the eyes."

"What's he going to show you with his eyes?" Lela asked.

"I'm sorry, but I can't help you."

"Oh, forget it. Come on," Annabelle said, and she pulled Lela away toward the produce section where a skinny pregnant woman in spandex pants was putting grapefruits into her cart.

"Excuse me. Do you know where the thing happened? A month ago? Do you know where it was in the store? I'm visiting from out of town."

The woman glanced down at Lela just as the man at the counter had. "I think it was in the parking lot."

"Where in the parking lot?"

"I don't know." She pushed her cart out of the produce section and disappeared around the end of the aisle.

"You promised me ice cream and a cookie," Lela said.

"Yes, yes." Annabelle didn't bother to mention that she'd said nothing about a cookie. When she turned around, the guy at the customer service desk was watching her as though she might cause trouble, and the idea of it was so ridiculous she considered for a moment walking right back up there and telling him as much. But Lela was impatient, tugging on her arm. So they got the ice cream and the bakery cookie—two actually (one for Annabelle as well).

At the checkout, Annabelle tried again.

The girl who scanned their items wore too much eye make-up and had a streak of blue in her hair. She said in answer to Annabelle's question, "I'm so happy you two lovely ladies came into my line!" She said, "These cookies look beautiful! As beautiful as the two of you!" She said, "Isn't our bakery the best?" She winked. Most likely, she was on drugs. Most likely, the wink meant nothing.

But Annabelle turned around and looked at the bakery again.

Lela did not want to return to the bakery section. "I'm cold. I'm tired."

"Just another minute. I promise." Annabelle tugged at Lela's arm, but Lela locked her knees, and so she staggered and then collapsed onto the floor.

"I'm so cold and tired, I can't stand up. I need you to carry me." She was on the floor right in front of the sliding glass doors, and people gave Annabelle dirty looks as they maneuvered their carts around her granddaughter's crumpled body.

"Lela, you have to get up. You're blocking the exit."

"You knocked me down."

"I did not. Come on, Baby."

"I'm too tired." Lela spread out on the floor as if she were going to go to sleep right there.

"You can't have ice cream and a cookie if you don't behave."

"You already promised me ice cream and a cookie."

Annabelle looked back toward the bakery section again. Colorful cakes, donuts, and cookies were arranged beneath sparkling panes of glass. No sign that anything out of the ordinary had happened there.

"OK, let's just go home, Pickle. Get up. Come on."

Lela said, "Because of you, that turtle is probably dead."

Annabelle stared at her granddaughter. She took a deep breath. "I'm sure the turtle is fine. Now, Lela, I can't carry you. You're a big girl. Get up."

"Mama would have saved it."

Before Annabelle could counter her, Lela screamed. An elderly man had walked by them with his cart, and now Lela was grabbing frantically at her head, and Annabelle saw strands of Lela's hair trailing from one of the cart's wheels.

Everyone in the store stared at Lela and at Annabelle.

The man from customer service appeared. He lifted Lela from the floor and deposited her a few yards away from the sliding doors. Lela quieted.

"Are you OK?" he said.

"My hair." She whimpered.

He said, "I'm sorry, but you shouldn't lie in front of the exit. You can't do that."

Then he looked at Annabelle. She could see he blamed her for Lela's fit. She saw Lela maybe three times a year at best, she wanted to tell him.

She said nothing, though. She simply took Lela's hand and led her out of the store.

Outside, the world had darkened. Annabelle could barely make out the outline of the mountains against the sky. She tried to imagine the sensation of a bullet passing through her skull. Swift like a streak of light through the dark. Jayde had said that as soon as a race is over, the pain of running it feels like a dream. Your legs are wobbly, your feet raw, but still you think you could have run faster, you should have run faster, and that the next time you will.

KEEPER FOUR

When the dying strikes the research facility, Keeper Four is alone in the bathroom. It happens quickly. Before, 58 employees are at the research facility. They are not all "at work." As Keeper Four will soon enough confirm when she makes her way through the building to assess the toll, the vice president dies while shopping online for yet another new pair of specs, the social media marketer while working on that memoir he's been writing for 15 years, one of the IT people with a thread of floss dangling from between her teeth. Keeper Four emerges from the bathroom to find bodies strewn about the floor and on chairs, like the scraps of food she offers the grizzly bear, SH90N8 (Sheena). The only other employee alive is one of the researchers. He is asleep seated at his desk—his head hung back, his mouth open. Keeper Four presumes he is dead, too, until he wakes from a noise of his own making—a cross between a snore and a hiccup. He stands, looks about the office, and curses.

Among the research subjects (referred to by the staff as "the residents"), only three remain. In addition to Sheena, both the girl, Y87EL2 (Yael), and the tiger cub, M13R4A (Mira) are alive. To give her and the researcher plenty of time to clean up the mess, Keeper Four sedates these latter two. Asleep, the girl's chubby arm wrapped around the tiger cub's soft middle, Yael and Mira look stuffed, as though they could be their own boxed display in the Field Museum. It's easy to overlook the rise and fall of their ribcages in the dim light. Keeper Four thinks of a circuit, only which is the battery and which the bulb? She pinches her right ear where there are two used-to-be holes that feel like tiny beads between her fingers.

Satisfied the sedative worked, that the pair will be asleep for hours, Keeper Four helps the researcher clear out the bodies. They carry the director out first—he the arms, she the legs. The director's skirt rides up her thighs, revealing a hidden tattoo: *Veni, vidi, vici* in calligraphy font, the words stacked on top of one another like cake tiers. Neither speaks of the tattoo. Neither speaks at all except to say, "Hold on, she's slipping" or "Can we move a little faster?"

Pitching the director's body into the Dumpster poses no particular challenge for Keeper Four. The same goes for their other coworkers' bodies. Only a woman with tiny pink braids sprinkled throughout her white-blonde hair gives Keeper Four pause. Because Keeper Four knows about the project manager's sensitivity to perfumes. Knows the project manager couldn't stand the sound of other people's breathing.

The Dumpster is full long before they finish, so they pile the other bodies behind the Dumpster where they will not be able to see them from the employee breakroom window.

The same goes for the bodies of the residents. They have to get creative with the animals that are too heavy to lift, like the hog, B713TY (Betty). They manage to, bit-by-bit, wedge a tarp beneath the hog's body then drag her out of the building. The process takes nearly forty minutes.

The director, if she were still alive, would not be surprised the tarp is the researcher's idea. The researcher is a lion—not literally, but figuratively. This according to the personality assessment they all had to complete upon employment. Aggressive and selfish, lions make good leaders, according to the director, also a lion.

Keeper Four is a fawn. Not simply a deer or even a doe, but a fawn, the computer monitor read. Agreeable, stubborn, clinical, passive, and indecisive: the five key traits of a fawn. Like sewing together five mismatched socks and calling it a glove. Fawns are also nurturing, according to the assessment. That's why they were assigned the task of caring for the residents— feeding them, comforting them, cleaning up their shit. They were assigned the jobs of being their mothers, according to Keeper One, the only one of the four keepers who actually was a mother. Keeper Two had self-identified as a dog mother. Whenever she went on about her one dog's anxiety issues or the other dog's habit of vomiting up moles and lizards onto her bed, talking about those dogs as though she was worried about their futures, as though, like Keeper One's human kids, they would need to eventually mature into responsible adults who would move out and care for themselves, Keeper One would roll her eyes.

Keeper Three had owned a hamster and kept a framed photo of the creature in a green St. Paddy's day top hat at her workstation, but other than that, she hadn't said much about the hamster.

Keeper Four, the surviving keeper, doesn't have any pets, has never had a pet, in fact. She was married once, to a man named Paul, but that ended because he started talking about making a baby.

All the keepers had suspected the answer that flagged them as nurturing fawns was the "cis female" bubble they'd each filled in. The only other employees at the facility who had uteruses, other than the director, were one of the copywriters and one of the researchers, both of whom would have marked something else: androgynous, agender, genderqueer, non-binary. Keeper Four is not fond of the "cis female" label. She is not particularly feminine. She doesn't wear skirts or dresses or make-up, doesn't get her hair highlighted or blow-dried, doesn't wax anything. She's never even owned a purse. Still, she understands that the very fact that the proliferation of gender labels has made her formerly stable identity feel unstable is evidence "cis female" is the only box she can conscionably check.

After receiving the results of the personality assessments, for several weeks they all had to walk around the facility wearing hats with the faces of their animals so they could "interact with one another in a more informed manner." For instance, fawns are not good goal setters, the director said, so there was no point in asking them what they thought. Better just to tell them what to do.

Still, as far as jobs go, there were worse things. She could have been assigned to clean up nuclear waste, for instance, or mine for radium, like Keeper One's sister.

What the employees at the facility who were sanctioned to think were interested in was interspecies relationships. Snakes forming friendships with mice offered to them as prey. Dogs nursing baby red pandas and piglets and wolf pups. There were so many stories like these. The researchers wanted to better understand what factors were at play. (Keeper Four had said once to her dear friend, Nina, that she wondered if the facility's long-term mission was to develop a drug that would induce maternal instinct. She'd said it as a joke, but once uttered, the idea seemed entirely credible, not a joke at all.) Why, for instance, did one dog happily accept a piglet into her care while another shunned the animal? Or worse. When the researchers offered a human baby to the grizzly bear, Sheena, the bear didn't just politely decline to mother the child.

This, by the way, was when Keeper One quit.

The other three were in it for the long haul, or at least they had been until four hours ago when Keeper Two turned white, collapsed, no pulse in her veins.

Along with the director and every other employee on shift, other than the surviving keeper and the researcher.

Concurrent with the dying, the internet went down, along with radio and phone service.

They'd all been informed this was coming—that is, the death-to-many part. Overpopulation, scarce resources, crumbling planet and all. They weren't told how or when, only that it would be quick and painless.

Years ago, when her friend Nina would say that given a little time, there's nothing that can't become normalized, Keeper Four would challenge her. "Nothing?"

The internet, radio, and phone service part is unexpected. That so many of her coworkers were taken, nearly all of them, is unexpected, too. Keeper Four believes something went wrong. Maybe there'd been some sort of miscalculation. She wonders if the facility is an anomaly or the norm. She suspects the latter.

Now, after removing the last of the deceased residents from the building, Keeper Four notes the night shift began forty minutes ago, yet none of the night employees have shown for their shifts, including Keeper Three.

No vehicles rumble past on the highway, either, which often she could hear when she stepped outside, if she was very still, put her ear to the wind.

Even the sky and trees seem empty of birds. Or maybe that's just coincidence. She does spot a lizard scurrying into a hole.

*

Keeper Four doesn't know whether to be grateful or devastated about Sheena. Grateful because they don't have to figure out a way to get her out of there. Grateful too because she's fond of the bear. Sheena never adapted to life in the facility the way so many residents seemed to adapt. She's still wild. Sometimes she'll open her mouth and let out a roar that makes the hairs on Keeper Four's arms stand on end.

Devastated because a day's worth of food for the grizzly is a day's worth of food for the rest of the survivors combined, and then some. There's surplus food in the residents' kitchen given the loss of the majority of the residents, but with no new food shipments expected now, they need to conserve as much as possible.

She could get in her car and try to drive back to her apartment, of course. No new paychecks expected, either. But there's nothing in her bare-bones apartment she misses. And the roads are most likely blocked from countless collisions. Not to mention, who knows what madness lies outside the facility? Better to stay put.

Also, the only person in the world whom Keeper Four loves, her friend Nina, is thousands of miles away, and very likely dead, and even if she is alive, how would Keeper Four know?

Yael and Mira and Sheena, on the other hand, need her. They'll starve if it's left up to the researcher.

"I say we terminate them," the researcher says after they've finished carrying out the bodies. He's standing before the fridge in the employee kitchen. He pries open a Tupperware container and sniffs the contents, zucchini lasagna that had belonged to the project manager. The project manager often brought in cakes or muffins she'd baked, always gluten-free and always moist and delicious. In fact, she'd brought in banana bread this morning, but nothing is left of it but crumbs on a white plate.

"You want to terminate me, too?" Keeper Four says.

"I wouldn't do that," the researcher says.

"I didn't ask if you *would*," she says.

The researcher complains about the lack of meat in the lasagna, but he eats every bite. Leaves the empty container in the sink below the sign that reads, *Please clean up after yourself by wiping counters and not leaving dishes in the sink. Your cooperation is appreciated. Management.*

Probably he doesn't know she is a vegetarian. The two haven't spoken more than a handful of short sentences to each other ever until today.

Probably he would have eaten the lasagna even if he had known.

Although they don't talk about it, Keeper Four knows the researcher is afraid, too. Otherwise, he would leave. Otherwise, he wouldn't have eaten a meatless lasagna.

"We're not killing them," she says.

"Fine, Fawn," the researcher says, "but you feed them from your half of the supply. Also, I call dibs on the leftover apple pie and all the frozen meals."

"You can't do that," she says.

"Everything in Walter's office is mine, too," the researcher says.

Keeper Four has no idea what of value is in Walter's office, which is on the east side of the facility. The east side is like Mexico to their state—close, but there's never been any reason for her to visit. She knows the assistant copy editor, from her side of the facility, recently replenished her snack drawers, though. She knows one of the IT guys has two candy jars and that there's rumored to be whiskey in the video editor's desk drawer.

She says, "I claim the west side of the facility. You can have the east. We split the fridge and the freezer evenly. If you don't like that, then leave. No one's holding you hostage."

The researcher smirks. He says, "Deal, Fawn. We split the residents' supply evenly, too. And I get the apple pie. And remember, if you insist on keeping them around, whatever you feed them comes from your half."

She says, "You would sooner let the four of us starve than share?"

"Don't get morally superior with me," the researcher says. "You eat less than me, I'm guessing. If it weren't for you choosing to feed the residents, you would easily be the one with the longer-lasting food supply. But instead of sharing that food with me, you're sharing it with them. You're choosing the residents over me."

She wonders if her protectiveness is largely selfish. She doesn't want to be alone in the world with only the researcher for company.

*

Keeper Four soon finds that Sheena is reluctant to eat. In the grizzly's habitat, she reaches her gloved hand into a white bucket containing a mix of sardines, berries, chopped carrots, and protein biscuits, and she conceals handfuls underneath anything she can find—a blue ball dotted with yellow stars, a couple of heavy boulders, a log. She rubs one of the sardines along the tops of these objects. Hiding the food is supposed to provide stimulation. The thrill of the hunt. But once she exits the enclosure and raises the gate that lets Sheena back into the area, the bear sniffs lazily at the boulders. Sheena grabs a mouthful from beneath the ball. Then she stops. Plops down beneath a tree. The director would say, *That's just Sheena for you.* Temperamental. Hard to please.

It's true Sheena is known to reject food, but this is a new level of temperamental.

Before this job, Keeper Four would have guessed finickiness was largely a human trait, more specifically, a first-world trait, born of excess. But she's learned in the last twenty-one months that finickiness isn't so much species-specific as individual-specific. Some individuals roll with the punches, take what they can get. They're adaptive. Others would sooner starve than compromise.

When Yael wakes, she nuzzles her face against Mira, then wipes her eyes. She sits up, looks around, signs, "Food." Keeper Four is relieved the researcher is not there to see. He'd start up again about ways to kill the child. "It doesn't have to be cruel," he'd said earlier. "You could drug a Snickers. She'd die happy."

Keeper Four raises her fist and nods it toward Yael, the sign for "Yes." She brings the girl a banana, her favorite. Keeper Four starts the unpeeling for Yael because otherwise the girl might struggle, cry. But she doesn't unpeel the banana completely and hand the inside to Yael undressed because Yael hates that, won't eat the banana. Yael wants to unpeel as much of it as possible by herself. In this regard, she is as finicky as Sheena.

Yael eats the banana and holds out the peel for Keeper Four to take and dispose. Then Yael signs "water," and Keeper Four hands her a sippy cup. The cups had been Keeper One's doing. She'd gotten Purchasing to order a dozen of them. They'd arrived in a crate packed four by three, each row of three a different color. "You can throw them onto the floor and not a drop leaks out. See?" Keeper One had demonstrated. It turned out the cups were handy with the monkeys, too.

When Yael is done with the sippy cup, she plays with a cloth doll that is Red Riding Hood, the grandmother, and the wolf all in one. You lift Red's skirt up over her head, and where legs should be, there is the wolf in grandmother's dress and cap. Turn the doll around, and there is the grandmother's face. Keeper One had brought in a couple of crates of old toys with which her kids no longer played.

Naming the residents had been the doing of the first three keepers. In the facility's records, the residents are only ever those series of numbers and letters, like a license plate or a flight record locater.

Keeper One had seemed to study Keeper Four sometimes. "I'm trying to figure you out," she said once. "You would have gone on referring to them as M13R4A and SH90N8 forever, I think."

Keeper Four probably would have, but she didn't see what was so remarkable.

"But then you go and bring Sheena a Honeycrisp apple from your house because she likes apples, and you say the Honeycrisps are better than the mealy apples the facility has in stock," Keeper One said.

Keeper Four said nothing.

"You never talk about yourself. We know nothing about you."

"I'm not a talker," Keeper Four said.

That wasn't entirely true. To Nina, she had talked plenty over twenty-plus years. But Nina was the one exception. Even when Keeper Four had been dating Paul, she hadn't talked much to him. Mostly they'd just rotated between three activities: fucking, eating, and television-watching, like those baby onesies that read, "Eat. Sleep. Poop." Even when she'd been married to Paul, there hadn't been a lot of talking, at least not until close to the end when he started up about producing a creature who could wear those onesies, and she responded that mothering was not in her nature. She'd pointed out a pigeon nesting in a tree in front of their house. What communicated that the flat bed of twigs was a nest was merely the pigeon's body posture, the way she squatted on the twigs. Anyone could see the nest was inadequate, that the eggs could easily roll out, and that even if they did not, once the eggs hatched, there'd be no walls to keep the babies from tumbling to the ground. "That's the kind of mother I'd be," she'd said to Paul.

Paul had argued with her, said that once she got pregnant, once she gave birth, she'd feel differently.

"You sound like one of those pro-baby advertisements," she'd told him. Despite all the talk about overpopulation and what to do about it, the push for women to fulfill their "natural role" had been as strong as ever.

Nina didn't argue with her. Nina loved her own kid fiercely, but she was frank about her ambivalence about being a mother. She talked about how she was constantly having to remind herself that there'd come a day when her time would be her own again. When Keeper Four told Nina about the pigeon, Nina said, "Having a kid is not something you should ever do for someone else. It's not like settling on calamari instead of nachos because Paul prefers calamari."

Nina was the only person who'd known about the pills Keeper Four took to prevent from getting pregnant. They weren't easy to come by anymore since they'd become illegal. She'd paid a lot of money for several years' supply.

*

Before the world as she knew it ended, Keeper Four had passed free time playing Minesweeper online. She enjoyed clicking a gray tile and watching as it and tiles around it disappeared, like water soaked up by cracked, parched soil. She was good at the game, too, patient and calculating. Now that there's no more Minesweeper, she shuffles food treasures about the west side of the building as though they're hidden mines her opponent, the researcher, wants to detonate.

Her efforts are validated when she catches him one afternoon in the assistant copy editor's workstation. She returns from feeding Yael and Mira, and there he is on her side of the building.

"What are you doing?" she says. *What are you doing in my territory?*

"I thought I heard something, like a rat maybe," the researcher says.

Keeper Four eyes the researcher's jean pockets for bulges.

"I didn't take anything, god," he says.

As soon as he's gone, she uses a ruler to push out the chocolates she keeps hidden inside the hollow sleeve of the copy editor's wrist rest. She transfers them to behind the coding books in the second developer's workspace.

She spends that entire afternoon relocating all her buried treasures. She doesn't eat them because she's saving them. She is investing in the perilous future.

But what is Sheena's strategy? Four days in and still Sheena hardly eats. Keeper Four brings a shovel into the bear's habitat and digs a hole. The dirt is tough, but with all her weight applied, the shovel breaks through. She deposits three sardines and pats the dirt down over them. She marks the spot with an additional sardine. When released into her habitat, Sheena eats the visible sardine lying on the dirt but then moseys over to a shady spot, plops down, and stares at the small, artificial stream. The bear doesn't even sniff the dirt.

Another day Keeper Four climbs the biggest tree in the grizzly habitat and strings sardines onto fishing wire that she found in the supply closet. She puts every last sardine from the bucket on that line. She hangs the line from the tree like tinsel. She stands back and admires her work.

But Sheena doesn't even look up. She sniffs at the berries hidden behind a log. The bear collapses onto the dirt and lazily chews lettuce leaves.

Keeper Four imagines rubbing her cheek against the bear's thick fur. Imagines lying beside the bear under that tree, listening to the animal's breathing. She also imagines Sheena ripping her apart limb by limb. She doesn't really think the bear would kill her, though. That baby had been so small. Keeper Four isn't small, nor is she so large as to be a threat.

Then again, you never can tell what will threaten another being. That evening, the researcher goes on again about the food supply. He says he's seen her wasting food, burying it in the dirt in Sheena's habitat, only he doesn't call it a habitat; he calls it an "enclosure." The word lodges in Keeper Four's ears like a foam plug. It's a little while before she hears anything else the researcher says.

Then she hears, "I think if you had to choose between that bear and me, you'd choose the bear," which reminds her of what Paul said in the end, that he thought she'd rather lose him than have a baby. These men and their warped sense of their own value.

She could say, "Why shouldn't I choose her over you?" but that will only make him angrier, paranoid, more of a threat to Sheena, Yael, and Mira. So she says instead, "I've been thinking I may need to release Sheena into the wild. She's not eating. I'm worried about her."

The truth is she doesn't really want to let Sheena go because she doesn't want to part with her, but it's true, too, that Sheena is not well. The bear's own depression or whatever it is that's afflicting the animal is hardly the only threat. The researcher will almost certainly kill Sheena if Keeper Four doesn't set the bear free.

"Release it?" he says. "Why not just put the animal out of her misery?" His face sets in an ugly grimace.

"You don't care about her misery," Keeper Four says.

"You saw what it did to that baby," the researcher says. "The question is why do you care about its misery?"

"She didn't ask for that baby," is all Keeper Four says.

*

The researcher insists on locking himself up with Yael and Mira and the tranquilizer gun while Keeper Four frees Sheena. He doesn't say Yael and Mira are his hostages, that he's keeping them close not so much so he can protect them, but so he can protect himself. But Keeper Four understands. She knows he knows that *if* she had any ideas about setting Sheena on him, she wouldn't follow through with Yael and Mira as potential casualties.

Even behind those bars, with his hostages and his tranquilizer gun, the researcher looks frightened.

"That bear's going to kill you," he says.

"Well, if she does, more food for you," Keeper Four says.

"Not if I can't get out of here because there's a bear terrorizing the facility," he says.

Of course, that's why he has the tranquilizer gun. He's got enough darts to put Sheena out for days, probably.

"Why would she want back in here once set free? To eat you?" she says.

She considers what her being mauled might mean for Yael and Mira. She hopes the researcher will not hurt them. She wishes the pair well. But she is no longer receiving a paycheck, and so those two are no longer her responsibility.

If the choice is hers to make, then she chooses Sheena. If Sheena does decide to maul her, then that will be Sheena's choice to make. But Keeper Four will not approach Sheena. She will keep her distance. She will not ask the bear to make any choice other than whether she wants to be free.

WINKELSUCHER

Oona's young son focuses the hand-me-down camera on his target, a yellow-bellied songbird perched on the stem of the tallest zinnia blossom in their garden. The pink zinnias rise like Seussian Truffula trees among the squat squash and melon plants.

"It's special," Max says of the bird. "I've never seen it before. Have you?"

Oona isn't sure. She's taken thousands of photos of this garden over the years, perhaps tens of thousands of Max. She photographs him now, in fact, as he adjusts the zoom lens. Like the bird, he doesn't notice yet that he's being watched.

He says, "It's still too far away."

"Then step closer. Slowly."

Max takes a tenuous step toward the bird, but it quickly flies away. Already Oona struggles to recall the details of the coloring on the bird's head and back. When she tries to locate it later in her bird book, she will be overwhelmed by the dozens of images of yellow-bellied songbirds.

Max drops his chin to his sternum. "I scared it."

She says, "Another bird will come if you're patient."

He says, "But I wanted that bird."

"I know," she says.

Every other Thursday after Max goes to bed, Oona and her friend Damon watch a double feature in her living room. Because Damon spent three years in graduate school studying film, before dropping out to teach yoga full time, he chooses the films. He pairs them carefully, like the wine and chocolate Oona selects for these evenings. Last night Damon paired a short documentary called *The Marina Experiment* with the horror film *Peeping Tom*.

She'd seen the latter in high school. Back then, they had watched movies at Damon's house. He had a television in the remodeled basement that functioned as his bedroom. They could smoke pot and make out with boys, Damon and his boy on the bed and Oona and her boy on the worn blue sofa that smelled like sweat and potato chips.

She remembered well how the Mark Lewis character murders women, via a blade attachment, with the very camera with which he films them. She'd forgotten that Mark's scientist father had made him the subject of psychology experiments regarding fear's effects on the nervous system and so was always watching him, recording his responses to stimuli.

Therein lay one of Damon's pairing notes. *The Marina Experiment* is about Marina Lutz's discovery after her father died of many thousands of photographs, audiotapes, and films he took of her from birth to the age of sixteen. In one particular clip, Marina's father says, "Ah, look at this!" as he approaches an approximately twelve-year-old Marina from behind. She's in her underwear and is bent over a bed, busy with some task Oona can't make out. Marina jolts around. The look on her face is caustic. Watching the film, Oona felt as though that look was intended for her.

This is what Oona thinks of when in their garden Max looks up suddenly and catches her lens aimed at him.

He didn't used to mind her photographing him, but now he does—just as a few months ago, he loved avocado, but now a thin sliver of it on his plate elicits tears.

The look on his face is like Marina's in the film clip, only this time Oona's not a passive spectator.

She wants to say, you were trying to take a picture of that bird without its permission. Of course, he did not vow to the bird that he would honor its wish not to be photographed.

Marina Lutz's archive stands out among other family archives because her father sexualized her. According to Damon, the archive stands out, too, because of its enormity and because Marina wasn't a willing subject. "All those videos of her sleeping!"

But just yesterday, before Damon came over, Oona photographed Max when he fell asleep on the carpet. A sharp beam of sunlight from the window exposed the particles of dust swirling around his head like matter accreting to form the universe.

Photographing children often involves subterfuge. Helen Levitt, one of the greatest street photographers of all time, attached a device called a winkelsucher to her camera so she could face one direction, while stealthily focusing her camera lens in another. Oona earns the bulk of her income taking lifestyle photographs, which are semi-staged in such a way as to look candid. Between shots, the children's parents wave cookies like dog biscuits.

Not a day passes that Oona doesn't photograph Max. Every parent photographer she knows is the same. Why shouldn't they make their children the subjects of their art?

She said to Damon, "I don't think there's anything wrong with the volume. Documenting your children's lives is the norm these days. You've seen Viv's mommy blog. She could probably fill a book with that child's dialogue alone."

Damon groaned. "Don't start me on that. It's like Viv thinks that child's words hold the secrets to the universe."

"It's exactly like that," Oona said.

Damon studied her. "This family photography business has corrupted your brain cells. I miss the artsy, raunchy nudes."

"I still take artsy, raunchy nudes," she said. She told him about how her son once bent over, pulled his butt cheeks apart, and asked her to photograph his asshole. So he could see what it looked like. She'd conceded under the condition that they delete the photo immediately after he looked at it.

Damon nearly choked on his wine. "Not what I had in mind." Then he said, "But you wouldn't photograph him if he didn't want you to. You wouldn't treat him like the subject of an experiment."

Oona didn't correct Damon. She stuffed a chocolate into her mouth.

What she wanted to say was that all children are experiments—messy, uncontrolled, long-term experiments. Every day, there's more to observe and discover. Is it any wonder parents feel compelled, even entitled, to document?

Now, in the garden, the anger and betrayal on Max's face is not quite like anything Oona's seen there before. She quickly pushes the shutter-release button several times before lowering the camera, despite that he flinches as though each opening of the shutter were the prick of something sharp.

LIFECYCLE OF AN UNGRATEFUL DAUGHTER

Gestation

Your body was furnace, blowpipe, and wind. She was the fiery, molten, untouchable thing you had to work so carefully, the something at once exquisite and banal you shaped through a wash of chemicals and fire just as a mustached man had done the blue and white candy dish on your mantel, a memento from your honeymoon. You did the best you could to keep certain ingredients out—the depression that overcame you some days, that wet-feathered feeling, that dull emptiness (ironic considering your state) that if not kept in check might mallet out hollow deposits where organs should be.

She was hope, this tiny amoeba swimming in your belly, this fortune cookie. She was your impetus to free yourself of your own mother for good—for the sake of your unborn child.

Your husband probably said something like, "You won't do *that*. Only crazy people do that." His entire extended family lived in the same town—he and all his siblings within twelve miles of the house they grew up in. "Don't you tell me about crazy," you said to him. Or maybe you said nothing. Maybe you didn't speak to him for whole days.

Perhaps *she* became your confidant. You told her a story about a girl who was victim to a psychotic and cruel mother, a mother so wicked the child used to wish for magic to rescue her. Magic never did.

Not from any lack of effort on the girl's part to conjure it, though. She planted many a jellybean in hopes that one might grow a stalk straight through to another world. She fed birds and mice, any creature willing to eat what she had to offer, in hopes that they might reward her by transforming into a carriage that would escort her away. She grew her hair long in hopes that a prince would climb to her rescue.

A man did climb to her rescue, you told your unborn daughter. He was no prince, but she loved him, and they married. She left her mother's house, and there was no reason whatsoever she should ever go back there again. Returning of her own free will to take more of that woman's abuse, now *that* would be crazy.

As your daughter grew larger and more solid, you grew exhausted and weary. All your normal aches and pains—your migraines, allergies, and fatigue—seemed inflated, maxed out. Your head pounded so badly some days that the weight of your hair became unbearable, so you cut it off at your shoulders.

Like the first and only sweater you ever knitted, your daughter was a project with which you couldn't wait to be done. You never did finish that sweater—gave up before you got to the sleeves. Maybe you worried the same would happen to her—that your body would spit her out before she was ready. (Several years later—she couldn't have been more than about five—she came across that chunky green sweater torso, the needles still attached, in one of your crafting bins, and she unraveled it. Of course, she didn't understand why you were so angry.)

Other times, maybe you reminded yourself you were making her, not the other way around. She was a passive recipient of your good will. If you wanted, you could let the fire have her.

Birth

Finally, you were rid of her, only to receive her all over again. What was extraordinary was not that you made her, but that though the pain of expunging her was itself extraordinary, you took her back. And not because you had to. You took her into your arms, told her you wanted more than anything to be a good mother to her. Whatever she later might accuse you of, however she might feel jilted, you figured you would always have this: you never *had* to give her anything, but you gave her life out of the goodness of your own heart.

Second Week

Her skin was velvet ice cream. You could have left her out under the sun until she melted if you'd wanted. You were wickedly amused by the pleasure it gave you to have so much power over her, weren't you? That her survival depended on you? Power, you came to understand, is one of the joys of motherhood.

This revelation also depressed you. As a little girl you would probably have sacrificed a neighborhood cat if your mother would have embraced you tenderly just once, if she had kissed your cheek.

You vowed to give her everything you never had, everything you were capable of giving her at least.

If she said she wants to be a gymnast, you wouldn't tell her she'd probably just break something as clumsy as she was; you'd enroll her in gymnastics lessons if it meant you had to eat saltine crackers from dawn 'til dusk. You'd make pretty bows for her hair.

The two of you would plant beans in Styrofoam cups; pick out patterns for doll clothes; comb the beach with a metal detector, unearthing buried treasures.

Tenth Month

You could not say she wasn't a good baby. You'd heard the horror stories, and sometimes you wondered what you did right to deserve such an agreeable, quiet child. Karma, you decided—you'd suffered enough in your life. The least you should get was a good baby! However, you felt sometimes that she was judging you, sizing you up, that she found you utterly disappointing—when you checked her diaper for the fifth time, and she was clean still, and she looked peeved by your perverse need to keep peeking inside her pants; when she grabbed at the air, gesturing for something, and you gave her plastic rings, Cheerios, the dish rag in your hands, and, finally, she dropped her arms and head in that dejected way, as if she had too little faith in you to bother howling at the top of her lungs like other babies; when you were feeding her mashed carrots from a jar, and the carrots seeped out of her mouth and down her chin, and she sighed as if she was burned out, close to giving up on you entirely.

Third Year

She said "mama" and "dada" and a number of other words: chair, grass, ball, juice. But mostly she was silent. She spoke only when you asked her a question. And when you asked her questions simply to prompt her to speak, questions such as "What's your name?" and "Where's your bunny?" she seemed to know what you were up to. She refused to answer.

Then one evening after you put her to bed, she cried like a mad woman, and you and your husband went to her, and she said, "I want water." She went from single words to an entire sentence, just like that. Her dad was impressed by her leap. You'd never see a bigger grin on that man's face.

You concluded that she was holding back from you all that time because she wanted to get it right. She was practicing in her head. She didn't want to make a mistake in front of you. She didn't want to give you the pleasure of working with her, seeing her try and fail and improve. You came to think of this as her first big betrayal. You would not say that to her when you recounted this moment several years later, but she would sense the resentment lurking behind your amusement.

Fourth Year

Already, she acted like she didn't need you anymore. She wanted to do everything herself. If you tried to brush hair out of her face, she wiggled herself out of your grip. If you tried to put shoes on her feet, she squirmed.

But who prepared the food she stuffed into her mouth all by herself? Who washed the laundry so she didn't run around in her own stink? Who got the temperature of her bath water just right, so she wasn't too hot or too cold? Who had to get up from her coupon-cutting or ceramic-painting to put in a video for her to watch? Who took her to ballet class? Who turned on her nightlight every night because the button was too stiff for her fingers to maneuver?

Once, when you were into your third trimester with your second child, and you were so depressed you felt as heavy and stagnant as a sink full of soaking, dirty dishes, you closed the door to her bedroom while she was napping, and you sat on the couch, gritted your teeth, and quietly cried. You heard her hand struggling with the doorknob. It was a stiff, heavy door that your daughter hadn't yet mastered opening. You prayed she'd give up and go back to bed, but instead, she cried—screamed. It was the most terrible sound she'd ever made. Perhaps because she thought she didn't need you or perhaps because you felt so hopelessly in the pits, and you couldn't bear caring for another person, you ignored her for whole minutes—three? five? ten?—before running to her door and lifting her into your arms. Her clothing was wet from sweat and urine—she had been trying to get to the potty. As you brushed her damp hair away from her eyes, you told her that mommy was outside getting the mail and didn't hear her, and it would never happen again.

Her humiliation gave you a smidgen of pleasure.

If you had known this event would become her earliest memory, perhaps you would have gone to the door sooner. Or maybe you would have waited even longer. After all, it's dishonest and cruel of her to dwell on one unhappy incident among so many happy memories.

Sixth Year

Other parents marveled at how quiet and well-behaved she was, how dutiful. She read to her little brother and sister (there were three of them now), calming the little hellions down with animals that talked and flew rockets to marshmallow stars. She sorted socks and set the table for dinner.

At Target, you gave her and her brother five dollars spending money, and she chose a purple-inked pen that cost two dollars and gave the remaining three to her brother, who greedily snatched the bills from her hands. He wanted a toy that cost twenty dollars, and because he didn't have a grasp on numbers yet, he screamed and screamed until you gave in. As you lifted the toy from the shelf, your oldest pointed out that twenty was twelve more than eight, and you told her he was a baby and didn't understand. She, a not quite six-year-old kid, said, "Isn't that spoiling him?" To shut her up you offered her ten more dollars, but she refused. Perhaps you took some pride in her selflessness. Proof of your good parenting? But certainly you resented her for it. She was trying to shame you! She was calling you a bad mother!

Ninth Year

Other kids, your two youngest included, as well as every cousin and every kid on the street, lived to perform for adults, but not her. All she wanted to do was read and write in her journal, a yellow, spiral-bound notebook she kept in her pajama drawer. Its pages were not filled with what she did on a given day or what boy she liked or how she hated you for making her share with her brother and sister the paints she received for her birthday. In it, you found entries about how it might be possible to travel in time, whether or not plants can feel, an imagining of what it would physically feel like to have her head severed from her body but both body and head still alive. Though you certainly couldn't say what was so smart about any of this, you knew you certainly never had any such journal; and you sensed that this bizarre journal was evidence somehow that she *was* smarter than you. Either that or she might be psychotic.

You found yourself nudging her to play with other kids—
to perform comedy acts and reenactments of battles from
space invader movies, to dance and sing and do cartwheels,
but she seemed irritated and humiliated by your suggestions
she join the other kids in their nitwit activities. Maybe you
wondered why you pushed her to play with other kids when
you were never a joiner, either. Perhaps she was more like you
than you'd thought. Perhaps you would have been like her,
reading and writing weird stuff, if your family had nurtured
and encouraged you the way you do her, if you hadn't had to
spend your childhood tiptoeing around your alcoholic and cruel
mother, if your mother hadn't killed any creativity you had by
constantly declaring you incompetent.

Perhaps. What you could say for certain was your daughter
was not the ideal companion you'd hoped for, far from it. She
didn't ask why, why, why like your other two kids—which could
be annoying for sure, but at least they looked to you for answers.
She supplied answers to questions you didn't ask. "The reason
that woman was looking at you like that is because Natty kept
trying to grab things in her cart and all you did was tell her to
stop it. You should have apologized, Mom." And "A brown recluse
bite probably isn't going to kill you. The poison kills the tissue
around the bite and causes nerve damage, but that's it." The
only questions she asked you for the answers to were: "Why do
you sleep so much?" and "Why do you always have headaches?"

Once, you asked her about her journal. You asked what
would make her wonder about what it would feel like to have
her head severed from her body. But she wouldn't let you into

her world. She looked at you with contempt and said simply, with such fire it stunned you, "I don't touch your things, so don't touch mine."

You vowed to never again try to get inside her head. To never again put yourself at her mercy. To never again lay your heart on her chopping block.

Eleventh Year

For reasons you could not understand, her younger sister was in love with her. Your youngest would sacrifice television, cake batter, and the plastic horses she adored just to be in the vicinity of her older sister. But your oldest didn't reciprocate this affection. This you did understand. Your youngest child unwittingly ruined everything. She put her sticky hands on your oldest daughter's books and on her green satin jewelry box. She broke the sand dollar given to your oldest by her Uncle Ivan who lived on the beach. She made scuff marks on your oldest daughter's favorite pair of shoes, white patent leather Mary Janes. All that and your youngest child was agonizingly dependent and whiny, the opposite of your oldest child. You were relieved by her interest in her older sister and you encouraged it—"Why don't you go look for your sister?"—because sending her after your oldest was the only way to get a few minutes of peace for yourself. You ordered your firstborn to take the youngest with her bike riding, and when she scowled at you, you told her she was selfish. She said, "She's *your* kid. You gave birth to her, not me." "That's right," you said. "And I gave life to you, too, and I can take it away if you keep giving me lip." She rolled her eyes at you for repeating this tired statement yet again.

The problem was that your oldest knew how to get even with you when you unloaded the burden of your youngest daughter on her. She didn't hit her, she quizzed her. And your youngest was unable to correctly answer any of the questions posed to her. "How many planets are in our solar system?" "Five." "What's fifteen minus seven?" "Seven." "What's the colored part of your eye called?" "Pupil." "What are you, an idiot?" Then your baby cried, and you had to console her. "It's your fault," your oldest daughter said. "You shouldn't let her watch so much television. You shouldn't treat her like a baby." You told her she was a bully.

When report cards came home again, and your oldest received thirty game tokens for her straight A's and wouldn't share any with her siblings, who didn't receive any tokens because those cheap bastards at the arcade changed to an all or nothing policy, you relished the shock on her face when you bought your other two kids thirty tokens apiece plus five more each to top her. You wouldn't be a good mother if you didn't take up for your younger children, if you didn't protect them from her.

And you *are* a good mother. Every penny you got your hands on back then went to your kids. And it wasn't easy to provide for your kids—their father was as cheap as they come. It's not that he didn't love his children, but he could care less whether they went to school in worn-down, ragamuffin clothes. You had to fight him every year for adequate money for their school clothes.

You had to practically wrestle money from him. And when that wasn't enough, you scraped up whatever little leftovers you could after groceries and gasoline and doctor's appointments.

You aren't just a good mother, you are a wonderful mother! You filled the pantry with chips and snack cakes and all their favorite cereals—everything in cheery-colored packages. Filled the fridge with canned sodas, juice boxes, and string cheese. Bought the kids pets—hamsters, guinea pigs, parakeets, and turtles—when their father told them if they wanted pets, they should play with the squirrels in the trees and the crawdads in the ditches.

You sewed doll clothes, painted ceramic sleeping kittens and dancing ballerinas for their dressers. On holidays, you decorated cupcakes for them to take to school for their classmates. Decorated the house, too—put up cobwebs and plastic skeletons for Halloween. One year you made a life-size Frankenstein that you propped up in a wicker chair on the front porch, until someone—you eyed your oldest daughter with suspicion—decapitated it, and so you threw its remains into the garbage.

Fourteenth Year

She was a pimply, brace-faced, gawky-kneed, bad-hair teenager. Some days you relished her suffering. Karma. Other days, you did everything in your power to help her out. You took her to pierce her ears, even though her father said not until she's twenty. You took her to buy make-up, even though her father said not until she's thirty. You bought her a sparkly silver gown for her freshman-year dance, even though it cost forty dollars more than the budget you and her father agreed on.

The one thing she had going for her appearance was she was thin, whereas the pediatrician said her little sister, only nine years old, needed to lose fifteen pounds. You tried to restrict your youngest from eating fattening, sugar-laden foods, but she looked so longingly at her older sister's and brother's plates, and both of them grinned so happily, cruelly as they ate their donuts or pastry tarts that you would cheat and give your little one a donut, too, or a chocolate bar or a bag of chips. Your son said, "I thought she was on a diet." You said, "She just needs to lose a few pounds. And mind your own business." Then your oldest said, "You think you're being nice to her by giving her that donut, but really you're hurting her." Your youngest cried, and you screamed at your oldest daughter to get out of your sight before you killed her.

Around this time, you got an idea, perhaps from a daytime talk show, to get your family together one night a week to talk—to get to know each other better, to become closer as a family. On the first Sunday night, you suggested everyone share a desire they have. Your youngest went first—she wished for a puppy, though she knew her father had forbidden it. Your son said he wished for a four-wheeler. Your oldest daughter wished the rest of you would read a book once in a while or paint or take up darts or working on cars, anything but wasting your lives watching television. Your husband wished he'd win the lottery because at the rate you all spend money, he'd end up working at Wal-Mart when he's seventy just to save himself from starving. You said you wished you knew how to play piano, to which your oldest replied that that was a great idea. She offered to help you find a teacher, to which you replied that you didn't have time or money to learn piano. Somehow her eagerness to get you playing Chopin made you want to strangle her, didn't it?. Why was that? Perhaps you were alike in your refusals to accept help from each other?

There were no more Sunday family meetings. None of you ever mentioned them again. It was as though it never happened.

Seventeenth Year

You didn't see much of her from here on out. She had club meetings after school, then work at the movie theater making popcorn and filling soda cups, and whatever time she had left over she spent at friends' houses and god knows where else.

None of you ate dinner together anymore. At most, you cooked once or twice a week. Whoever was around ate, and for whoever wasn't, you left the leftovers out on the stove. Other nights, you brought home fried chicken or burgers. Or else, you foraged in the freezer or the pantry or the fridge—a frozen pizza, a can of tuna, a chunk of watermelon.

You smelled cigarette smoke on her on those nights you were still awake when she came home. Sometimes you thought you smelled stale beer and marijuana in the house, but you could never tell where the smells were coming from—her room or your son's. He also smelled like cigarettes in those days. You felt helpless to stop them from drinking and smoking, or whatever else it was they did, so you pretended to be none the wiser.

Your son got arrested three times that year for petty theft. Your oldest daughter showed up on a Sunday morning with a bag of donuts and kolaches, and you didn't know whether she'd left the house before the rest of you woke or if she'd spent that night elsewhere. You didn't ask.

Your husband took up weightlifting. He started out going to the gym a couple of times a week, but before you knew it, he headed straight to the gym every day after work, not returning home until eight o'clock some nights, sweat-soaked and smelling of salt. He lost twenty pounds, and you no longer recognized his body when he traveled from the bathroom to bed in his boxer shorts. He had an affair with a woman from his gym, a nutrition consultant. You discovered her card in his underwear drawer, her cell phone number scrawled out on the back. You wanted him to tell the kids what he'd done, and when he called you crazy, you told them yourself while he was in the shower. Your youngest cried, the other two hugged you. You were like a real family for once, except for the absence of your husband, probably washing off evidence of his vitamin-laden mistress.

Nineteenth Year

She called to thank you for a package of Halloween treats you sent to her at college. You received a package, too, not directly from her, but from her school's Psychology department—a questionnaire you were asked to fill out in order to help psychologists study families with a history of depression. The letter accompanying the questionnaire explained that by participating, you would be helping your daughter complete her quota of research projects she had to participate in as a component of her grade in her Psychology 101 course. You did not mention this package because it embarrassed and angered you and because you had already disposed of it. You'd done enough to support her. You'd protected her from your mother, so that she didn't see just how bad depression could get. Maybe you believed there was nothing she'd ever needed that you hadn't made sure she had.

Or did you know that wasn't true? Did you know but felt incapable of giving anything more? Maybe all you could see was what she had that you had not.

Thus, you believed you deserved a thank you for all of that—a thank you for giving her a good home, so she could grow up to amount to something; a thank you for the money it would cost to house and feed her through four years of that fancy college (the scholarship didn't cover everything); a thank you for spending every extra penny you had on your children, so their lives could be better than yours. You wanted her to realize she'd had so many opportunities you never did—that it was not simply that you were dumb or country. You wanted some credit for who she'd become and all that she'd accomplished. She wouldn't be anywhere today if you had let her melt in the sun like an ice cream cone when she was several weeks old. If you'd drank your pain away like your mother, instead of taking anti-depressants and sleeping pills. You could have.

But what you got were tidbits about courses you wouldn't have dreamed existed—Anthropology of Sexuality, Psychology of Humor, Queer Disturbances in Nineteenth Century British Literature.

Her life was spooling into itself, growing hardier and tougher by the minute. Your life, which was never as hardy as hers was already, was spooling out all over the place. You tried to tell her this on the telephone. You told her you suspected her dad was having another affair. He was taking scuba diving classes now. When the training was over, his class would take a boat out to sea to scuba for real. You were not invited.

Your daughter asked what made you think he was having another affair—had anything suspicious happened? "Don't you take his side," you said. That man cheated on you, and after all you've done for him and for this family. "I'm not taking anybody's side," she said, and that was a slap in the face. She should take your side, of course. *You* were the victim.

Twenty-second Year

Somewhere along the line, between all those courses with complicated names, she announced she was going to be a fiction writer—not a doctor, not a lawyer, not an accountant, but a writer. Not even a newspaper journalist, which is what you thought when she first uttered the word writer. She wanted to write stories. Not horror stories or romance stories or children's stories, but literary stories, she called them. Immediately, you were nervous. What are these stories about, you asked. Are you in them?

"I don't know," she said, and there you had your answer.

Several weeks after the family drove twenty hours to attend her college graduation, you and her father filed for divorce. Turned out he was having another affair, and he was in love with this one. Your son would be a junior in college, and the youngest would be starting community college the next fall, so one week after that you packed what you could into your van, and you moved twenty hours away from home, too, except she went east and you went west.

Since she'd left home, you'd mostly waited for her to call you because you felt nervous somehow calling her. You never had anything to talk about, except the problems you'd been having with her father, which she didn't want to hear about. You were nervous, too, perhaps about her roommate answering the phone. Maybe you worried your voice would provide evidence somehow of mean things your daughter may have said about you.

So you waited until you settled into your new home, an apartment not so far outside of Los Angeles, before you called and told her about the divorce and your move. You felt like you'd gone off to college, too, you said, because you'd never been on your own before. You moved straight from your parents' house into a house with her father. It was like you were starting life all over again. She said she was proud of you and excited for you, and you thought, finally, she's on your side. You asked her to spend Christmas with you. You'd fly her brother and sister out as well. You'd all explore Los Angeles together. You'd sit on sidewalk benches and count celebrities.

Your son chose to spend his Christmas with a friend he met in college. The boy's family had money and a vacation home in Hilton Head. He was so excited, there was nothing to say. Your youngest couldn't bear to break the tradition of spending Christmas with her father's family. You were so depressed about your other children not spending Christmas with you that when your oldest arrived early on Christmas Eve, you told her you'd been feeling awful, that you may have a stomach virus, and that you'd have to pick up something from a drive-thru for Christmas Eve dinner instead of going into LA for the evening. She suggested you watch a movie together then, which you said yes to, but you changed your mind when you returned to the apartment. You felt just miserable, you said. You spent the entire four days of her visit in bed. You gave her the keys to your van and told her she could explore LA without you.

The two of you spoke only twice, briefly, over the next several years.

Twenty-fifth Year

You moved again, this time to Reno. She sent you an e-mail to say she'd be publishing her first story. She said she tried calling, but the line was disconnected. Did you change your number? Did you move apartments?

You e-mailed back to say you didn't think it mattered to her where you were since you never heard from her, not even on your birthday. She pointed out that you hadn't communicated with her except for on her birthday, and then only to send a card with a fifty-dollar check and a short message that you loved her and missed her. "Writing to me once a year that you love me and miss me and then disappearing isn't love," she wrote. "It is too," you wrote. "Don't you tell me I don't love you. You don't know the first thing about not being loved by your parents."

You congratulated her on her publication then asked whether she'd told her father about it. Yes, she replied, and when she told you that she'd told him first, it stung. You told her about how awful he'd been treating you, how he practically threw your belongings out the door when you went back to pick up some things you'd left behind, and not only was he cruel to you (*He* called *you* a bad parent! He said you needed to call your children more, as if he knows anything about what goes on between you and your kids!), but he threw her and her siblings' baby books at you like they were trash and like he didn't care about any of you at all, like this family never existed, never happened.

Again, she said she didn't want to talk about him. She said that if her father didn't care about her then he wouldn't call every couple of weeks. And he never talked about you, she said, as if the fact that he'd erased you from his life was proof of his benevolence. You were so tired of how her father could do no wrong. So tired of her defending him.

The problem was she was just like her father, you told her. You said you'd tried to be a good mother to her no matter how cruel she was. But like her father, she thought she was smarter than you, better than you. She acted like you were immoral and petty for talking bad about him when he was the one who cheated. That's what killed you, you said: how they both acted like they were on some higher moral plane than you.

You told her she was cold and heartless, and she always had been.

She hung up on you. Then she wrote you an essay practically about how you must not know her at all if you thought that about her and how it has hurt her to hear such things from you throughout her life. She said she loved you dearly, but you didn't make it easy to love you. This she said to her own mother, to you who have given her a world of things and opportunities you never had, who knows what a bad mother is, and who did the very best you could. You deleted the e-mail without finishing it.

You didn't reply.

You called her at Christmas, but at five in the morning, so as to get her voicemail. After the beep, you wished her a merry Christmas, and you said you loved her more than she would ever know. You let her return call go to voicemail. She said, "If you love me so much, why can't I ever know? What does that mean, Mom?" Damn her, you probably thought. Doesn't she know that the ordinary people of the world aren't so fucking literal?

Twenty-sixth Year

And then one day you received a package from her—a brown envelope containing a little book in which was printed her story, the one she'd told you about. A note included said she hoped the story would communicate what she never could in a straightforward conversation with you.

You dropped the magazine on your kitchen counter, and you didn't lay a finger on it for one whole day. You tried to forget it was there, but it was as if everything in your kitchen was orbiting around it, via centrifugal force.

The story was about you, sure enough. Most of what happened in the story wasn't really true. It didn't happen at all or it didn't happen exactly the way your daughter wrote it. And yet, you recognized through her humiliating familiarity that the mother in the story wasn't just what your daughter thought of you, but she *was* you—a distorted image, manipulated, but still you. It was as though your daughter had peeled you apart. The mother character in the story was a collage of your sharp edges and waxy panes.

You knew well enough you had faults just as much as the next guy. But so did your daughter, so what right did she have to go pointing yours out to the entire world?

You hit a point where you couldn't take even one more word. You got the unnerving feeling the end of the story would be the end of you—that when the characters had played out their roles, and the text broke off into blank space, something awful would happen to you. It was as if the mother in the story was a voodoo doll made in your likeness. The only way to save yourself from suffering whatever terrible fate that may await the character was to stop reading and close the book. So you did, and you ripped out the pages and shredded them into a hundred scraps, so that if someone were to rummage through your garbage, they couldn't possibly put the pieces back together again.

THE NATURAL
ORDER OF THINGS

The woman seated next to me on the plane says she's on her way to visit her son who lives in a group home. Her son is forty years old but has the mind of a two-year-old.

Like a kiosk worker peddling perfume in the mall, she offers up this information about her son without my asking. We're flying over the Grand Canyon, which looks like a scab from up here. My husband, Wade, is in the aisle seat across from us, watching a movie on his tablet. My six-year-old son, Henry, is in the aisle seat next to me, watching a movie on his tablet. I don't have a tablet. I have a book opened on my lap, my finger holding the sentence to which I hope to return.

My seat neighbor tells me her son's two roommates have minds equivalent to a seven-year-old and a twelve-year-old.

I think of how my son—six in mind and body, to the best of my knowledge—can never keep straight how a cat's age compares to human age, of our eighteen-year-old cat who is so bony that petting him is awkward, nerve-racking, in fact, like stroking the tangle of cords spiraling out from behind a hard drive. One day my son says, "So if he were human, he'd be three?" Another day he says, "So in cat years, I'd be ninety?"

My seat neighbor takes her son and his two roommates out to dinner at Golden Corral every time she visits.

She says, "I always go over the rules with them beforehand. I say, 'What are the rules?' And they say, 'One: Don't eat so much we puke. Two: Eat our greens before we have dessert.'"

The first time she took them to Golden Corral, all three of the men (children?) ate so much they puked.

I smile as though this is a charming anecdote because she smiles as though this is a charming anecdote, but the only instances in which I've heard of humans puking from eating too much concern drastic changes in food availability. Our younger cat, on the other hand, quite often pukes after eating. He scarfs his wet food up faster than I can refill his water bowl.

"I try to visit every four months," the woman says. "But sometimes I do surprise visits. You have to, you know." She doesn't say any more on this subject.

I nod. Who hasn't heard stories about neglect in places like that? Then I lift the black foam covering Henry's right ear and ask him if he needs a snack. He shakes his head in irritation, bats away my hand. His eyes never leave the tablet screen.

My seat neighbor smiles. "Independent."

"*He* thinks so," I say.

Soon she is telling me about her son's girlfriend. Because her son doesn't speak, his and his girlfriend's relationship consists of sitting next to each other and smiling. "They're adorable," she says.

I want to ask about her son's girlfriend's mind age and body age, but I'm afraid the answers might disturb me.

No matter the woman's son's girlfriend's mind age, if her body has been alive fewer than say thirty years, then this woman's son has no business sitting next to her and smiling, I think. But maybe I'm wrong, like I was wrong about how cats age compared to humans. Turns out that whole cats-age-seven-human-years-for-every-calendar-year thing is bogus. In general, cats age fast, then a little less fast, then less fast still. If you're into numbers, the average cat supposedly ages about five human years in a calendar year after reaching adulthood.

But "human years" is hardly a standard unit of measurement.

In his book *Ageless Body, Timeless Mind*, Deepak Chopra makes the point that people's bodies age differently. When I told Wade this, he said, "And for this he has a book?" But I don't think Chopra's point is as common knowledge as Wade suggests. At my gym, they calculate everyone's heart rate maximums using the same one-size-fits-all formula everyone everywhere uses. When the instructor tells us to run as fast as we can on those treadmills, to "empty our tanks," my heart rate monitor will report that my heart is beating at 102 percent, once as high as 105 percent, of my maximum heart rate, which is obviously untrue or else I'd be dead.

Then there's my sister Rita, four years my junior, who is always mistook by strangers, and even our Great Aunt Pammy, as the eldest. She's a stress junkie is why. That and she dumps Doritos and mixed nuts onto a plate and calls it dinner. The way she drags her feet, she looks as though she expects, and maybe wants, to die any day now.

Our older cat reminds me of Rita. Because he no longer grooms himself, his fur has become matted and clumpy. I snip away these clumps from time to time, leaving behind nearly-bald patches. Sometimes the clumps loosen all on their own. We find them on the floor, the sofa, in the litter box. His fur babies, we call them. Rothko's claws don't grow right anymore, either. They're thick and dull, no fine points.

One evening a few weeks back, he squatted in our bathroom while we were brushing our teeth before bed. Squatted like he was going to poop right there on the tile by the shower. He did that for maybe ten seconds, then stood, took a few steps, and squatted again. Nothing to show for his efforts. But the next morning, we found three hard balls of poop scattered about our living room like the younger cat's toys. Rothko slept all day. Didn't even get up when I jiggled the treat bag. I checked him periodically to make sure he was still breathing.

Every time we leave town now, I worry the cat sitter will arrive to find Rothko dead. I don't mean I think it would be such a terrible thing for him to die. His senses are so gone, he's always getting beneath my feet. Every day it's an effort not to step on him. What I think in these close calls is what if I were geriatric, too? I'd either end up killing him by stepping on him or killing myself in my effort to avoid stepping on him. Living with a very old cat means constantly contemplating your own mortality, your own impending frailty. I mean, I worry because it would be awkward for the cat sitter. Would she wrap him in a plastic bag? Then what?

My son wants little to do with Rothko anymore. His refusal to brush that cat makes me think of Eskimos, how they supposedly used to send their elderly adrift to die on ice floats. I read that in actuality, senilicide was rare, a thing that happened only during times of famine. And when it did happen, it wasn't nearly so picturesque. They just stopped feeding their elderly. Or they locked them out of the house in the cold.

My son used to cuddle that cat. He doesn't remember, though. Three years is half his life ago. When we boarded the plane an hour ago, he said he loved the cinnamon-flavored pastry tart I fed him for breakfast the day before, and could he have one again sometime soon, and I corrected him. "That was this morning," I said.

His time confusion extends to me. Last year, when I was forty-five, he asked me no fewer than a hundred times how old I was. "How old are you again? I forgot." Sometimes when I answered him, he'd say, "What?! I thought you were fifty-five" or, "I thought you were sixty-five."

Another point Deepak Chopra makes in that book is the body is mostly water, and there is no such thing as old water. But when I answered my son's question with "I'm as old as water," his eyes grew wide. He said that because water cycles, it's all super old.

I have a friend who is often saying, "Growing old is hell." Between my cat and her mother's dementia, our conversations almost always circle back to aging and death. Also, her partner had a stroke a couple years back, at the age of forty-six. He's fine, fully recovered, but the shock of it is not something any of us has recovered from. He's just about the healthiest man I know. Goes to the gym every day, drinks kale smoothies for breakfast.

And now there's Wade's sister's eleven-year-old daughter, Savannah. Cystic fibrosis. "Complications," my sister-in-law said on the phone. That's why we're flying to Chicago, I tell my seat neighbor when she asks: for my niece's funeral.

My seat neighbor's blue-gray eyes glisten. She says, "I'm so sorry."

In a photograph taken on her eleventh birthday, Savannah looks to the ceiling over her hospital bed. It's pocked with plastic, glow-in-the-dark stars.

In my son's school, they celebrate birthdays with a ritual that makes me shiver every time I watch my son do it. The birthday child is presented with an inflatable globe the size of a soccer ball. The child carries Earth around the sun, represented by a lit candle. Triangular, yellow rays fan out from the candle's base, each triangle printed with the name of a calendar month. The child begins with his feet next to the month he was born. A chorus of children's voices count off the revolutions each time the child reaches that month again. I shiver, I think, because every year I realize I've lost track somehow of the tangible fact that age is measured by the movement of the planet.

It's not a wonder I forget this, what with the way we use age as a measuring unit for so much else, as though age were a direct measure of our abilities and accomplishments. One doesn't need an extreme example like my seat neighbor's son to know age is always a faulty measure for such qualities as maturity and intellect and vigor, or examples like my friend's husband or my niece Savannah to know disease and death can strike the young as well as the old.

Or maybe I shiver because every revolution is like another entry into the death raffle.

Wade said yesterday after his sister called that it's not the natural order of things for a parent to outlive a child.

The plane buckles through turbulent clouds. I check that my son's seatbelt is clasped. Then, though I know it's a useless gesture, I supplement the seatbelt with my arm. My son's only acknowledgment is a grumble and a shifting in his seat so that his view is unobstructed.

I think of the arrival of Gambel's quail chicks, a hallmark of spring in the desert where we live. Early in the season, I see parents leading as many as twelve fuzzy, gray chicks through the desert brush. Some weeks later, it's much more common to see parents leading just one chick, maybe two.

THREE-WEEK CHECKUP

The pediatric exam room had one window, and on the other side of that window a roadrunner looked in at Deena and the baby. Red, white, and blue stripes showed so brightly along the side of the roadrunner's head that Deena wondered if the bird's feathers concealed fifty tiny white stars. Deena felt that the roadrunner was not only watching her but listening. This feeling of being monitored always was not new exactly. In the last couple months of pregnancy, twice she'd had to collect all of her urine for a 24-hour period into a thick plastic pouch that had resembled a Camelback hydration pack, otherwise known as a bladder. During the labor, when she'd done some of the pushing in a warm tub, a nurse had, without a word, scooped escaped turds with a small aquarium net designed for transferring goldfish. Also, the midwife had checked the baby's heart rate over and over to make sure he was "coping with"

Deena's "long labor." The midwife's words had made Deena feel like a child being told that her prolonged piano practice time was her own fault because she kept getting distracted, doing shit other than playing piano. And then there was the way the midwife scolded her as the baby was finally crowning: "You've got to push harder than that, Deena. Stop holding back."

A show Deena watched sometimes on television, a show about human psychology, often showed video clips of adults and children both caught through a one-way mirror doing the thing they'd been instructed not to do: getting up from the chair, checking the cell phone, sneaking frosting from the cake. This is what Deena thought of when the nurse entered the exam room and began her cross-examination with the question, "Are you breastfeeding?" Of course, Deena knew the correct answer. She was grateful she didn't have to think about this one, make a decision about whether to lie or embellish. A breast pad was stuck to her left nipple. She could smell the sweet funk of her milk, a scent something like a halved cantaloupe that had been left inside a parked car on a hot day. The nurse could probably smell it, too. As if this weren't evidence enough, the baby was asleep at her right breast, his mouth still clasped tight around her nipple. She thought of her friend Hazel's online shop, Bootyque, on which Hazel sold pretty, beaded nipple clamps she made by hand. Deena had tried on a pair of those clamps once, before she got pregnant, before breastfeeding. Hazel's clamps were to her baby's latch like umbrella'd pink drinks to a straight shot of whiskey.

When the nurse asked Deena if she breastfed at night, Deena said, "Does a cow—" Then she stopped. What she had meant to say about cows and what it had to do with breastfeeding at night, she wasn't sure. Her words rarely came out right anymore. When she'd spoken to her mother-in-law on the phone that morning, she'd felt as conspicuously incoherent as when she'd shown up to work for her grocery cashier job in high school still tripping on acid she'd taken the night before.

The nurse looked confused.

Deena said, "Yes, yes. I breastfeed at night." She smiled. The nurse smiled.

But Deena's smile was weak, self-conscious. Because the nurse seemed to Deena like an interviewer, the way she sat above Deena on that red swivel stool, typing words Deena couldn't see into a laptop. In the fluorescent lights of the pediatrician's office, Deena felt wholly unqualified for the position for which she was applying.

In the privacy of her home, when it was just Deena and the baby, she was comfortable enough, certainly not inadequate. The only serious hindrance was her exhaustion. She felt undone by her exhaustion, as though her body were a disassembled pile of pieces that a first-year med student had been tasked with putting back together again to assess her mastery of anatomy and physiology. The student in question had not paid close attention in class, had not read her textbooks or studied the diagrams. Deena could hardly walk without bumping into things. It was a wonder she hadn't dropped the baby or smashed his head into a door.

The nurse asked, "How many times in a given night do you breastfeed?"

This was an example of the other type of question the pediatrician and pediatric nurses asked: ridiculous questions that were impossible to answer.

Deena stared stupidly at the nurse. "You want a count?"

"It doesn't have to be exact," the nurse said. "How many times approximately?"

"What constitutes night?" Deena asked.

The nurse stared at her. "How about this: What is the maximum number of hours you'd say the baby goes without breastfeeding?"

"Hours?" Deena said. "Whole hours?"

The nurse seemed satisfied and asked no more questions about breastfeeding.

*

When the pediatrician entered the examination room, he sat on the stool and rolled over toward Deena. He said, "Let's take a look at those ears, little man." She held the baby out toward him, but he said, "Just hold him up for me." Then he leaned in so close that she felt self-conscious about the sound of her own breathing. The pediatrician was handsome—not her type, but handsome all the same. His hair was longish, fluffy, and she had to resist the urge to reach out and touch it.

When the pediatrician was done with his examination, he rolled over to the same laptop the nurse had typed into. He said, "How often does he have bowel movements?"

Deena felt sure she was blushing. The pediatrician didn't beat around the bush.

She wanted to point out that it wasn't a fair question, that she didn't change all the diapers—most, yes, but not all. Did the pediatrician assume that because Jeff couldn't make the appointment, Deena was the sort of woman who did everything while her partner relaxed in front of the television with a beer?

Deena wondered if she'd chosen her pediatrician poorly. The books had said she ought to interview a bunch of doctors, but there'd been so much to do already to get ready for the baby without driving around town in a car with a faulty air conditioner to interview doctors. And really, what questions would she have asked? How different could pediatricians be? Now she thought that the good pediatricians would not ask a woman with a three-week-old infant to try to remember something so ridiculous as the number of times her infant's bowels moved each day when she couldn't even remember to brush her teeth.

Deena said, "Six maybe? Two? I'm not sure."

The pediatrician typed something into the laptop. Then he looked back up and asked, "What are the baby's sleeping arrangements?"

"Sleeping arrangements?" Deena said, not comprehending.

"Does the baby sleep in a crib or a bassinet?" the pediatrician said.

Of course, the answer was that the baby slept on Deena's breast. Deena looked down at the baby, back up at the doctor.

Where else would the baby sleep when the baby had one of her nipples in his mouth 24 hours a day?

There was a correct answer to this question, and Deena sensed that "on my breast" was not it. But saying anything else seemed preposterous given the baby's current sleeping circumstances. Like swearing she'd brushed her teeth that morning though she'd been eating mints at the rate she did popcorn at a movie and trying to open her mouth as little as possible because her teeth felt like moss-covered stones in a stagnant pond.

*

On the phone, Jeff said, "You should have lied."

"Lying comes easily for you, doesn't it?" she said from their bed, the baby asleep on her nipple again. The nipple that wasn't currently in use was cracked and bleeding. She'd received nipple cream as a shower gift, petroleum jelly glorified by the elegant, pink pump that dispensed it, but the baby would spit her nipple out and howl if she didn't wash the cream off before presenting said nipple.

"Lying about where our baby sleeps is inconsequential," Jeff said. "Who cares what he thinks anyway?"

"Why do I bother going to these appointments if we don't care what he thinks?"

"Because it's illegal not to take a baby to the pediatrician for check-ups?" Jeff said.

"Is it?" she said. One more question to which she didn't know the correct answer. "And here I thought we took the baby to the pediatrician because we care about his welfare."

Jeff sighed.

"And what if I lied and the doctor could tell?" Deena said.

"How would he know?" Jeff said.

"I'm not a good liar," Deena said. She wanted to say something more, something about this feeling of always being watched, like even at this very moment, reclining on her bed with the baby asleep at her breast. Another roadrunner—or the same one?—stood on top of the wall at the edge of their backyard. The paranoid sensation that the animal could hear and comprehend her words was, even more than the shame at how crazy she'd sound, what kept Deena from saying more to Jeff.

"Everybody knows that plenty of people sleep with their babies," Jeff said. "Put the baby in the bassinet if this bothers you. I don't care."

Jeff had been sleeping on the guest bed since the day they'd come home from the hospital. He'd lasted maybe two hours in their bed that first night before he took his pillow and left. On their honeymoon, when they got stuck in traffic on the way out of town because of an accident on the highway, she'd said, "We're in this together. Relax. Let's make the best of it." But after a few minutes at a standstill, he'd slammed the dashboard with his fist.

"I'm so tired, I feel like I'm going to die," she said now.

"I hear you. If I don't get a good night's sleep, I'm a wreck," he said.

Once, early in their relationship, she'd woken in the middle of the night, wrapped her arms around Jeff from behind and started kissing his ear; he'd swatted her like she was a giant fly. This is what she wanted to do to Jeff now. Swat him against a countertop. Watch his disfigured legs twitch.

"Can I get you anything from the store?" Jeff said.

"Homemade chicken parmesan. Or spaghetti and meatballs. Or a lasagna."

Hazel had dropped off a loaf of zucchini bread the previous afternoon. Deena had screeched at Jeff when he'd started to cut a slice for himself. "That's mine," she'd said. "I'm practically starving to death. Hazel's the only person feeding me." He'd opened the pantry and motioned to the carton soup, then opened the freezer and pointed to the frozen meals stacked like lumber. She'd cried. He'd abandoned the zucchini bread.

"I can't cook. But I love you. And because I love you, I'll pick you up something from that Italian place on the way home," Jeff said.

"I'm starving now," Deena said.

"So eat the zucchini bread," Jeff said.

"I already finished it," she said.

"The entire loaf?"

"I told you I'm starving. I'm using up a good 500 calories or more a day feeding him."

"Text me your dinner order," he said. "I want a written record should you think you ordered something you didn't."

"I definitely said tomato basil," she said as she hung up.

What she didn't tell Jeff was that after she'd told the pediatrician that the baby slept on her breast, and after the pediatrician had said that this sleeping arrangement wasn't safe for the baby, that she might roll over onto the baby in her sleep and smother it, the pediatrician had then asked her whether Jeff was supporting her. He'd said, "Is your husband supporting you and the baby?"

Deena had said, "I work full time, too. I'm just on maternity leave."

The pediatrician had squinted his eyes at her, then said, "I mean, when he's home, is he helping care for the baby? Is he helping care for you so that you are able to care for the baby?"

"Define 'care,'" Deena had said and laughed.

The pediatrician hadn't laughed.

Neither did Deena tell Jeff about how outside the pediatrician's office, in the parking lot, the baby strapped into his car seat, she had covered her eyes and cried. Or how when she took her hands from her eyes, she'd had the strange sensation that it was not noon but midnight and that, in fact, the sun was here to stay. And how she thought that because there would be no more darkness ever again, the criminals would have to adapt to committing their crimes in the light, and how once they made this adaptation, no part of the human world would even present the illusion of being safe again.

*

In the afternoon, after the baby had woken and nursed on the cracked and bleeding nipple, Deena took the baby outside to sit on the front porch swing. He seemed to enjoy being outside, and she did, too. It was early April, not yet hot. The euphorbias were in bloom, each tiny green flower like a fanged throat. Butterflies and hummingbirds hovered. The baby looked out at the world with the kind of intensity Deena's nephew and niece reserved for television and video games, only the baby's expression was deadpan because he wasn't able to smile or laugh yet.

A roadrunner crossed the street from Deena's yard toward the bright, lavender-colored sage in the yard across the street. Was it the same roadrunner?

She said to the baby, "See the big bird running across the street? That's a roadrunner."

The elderly woman who lived next door, her name was Phyllis, came out then to water a potted aloe. She commented on the roadrunner, too—to Deena, not the baby. Deena wondered if Phyllis could even see the baby, if her eyesight wasn't so good. Most people couldn't seem to resist commenting on the baby.

"I never get tired of seeing them," Phyllis said of the roadrunner, and Deena thought about what a strange phrase this was. The real risk of the commonplace was that you might stop seeing the thing at all.

Deena said, "They're funny birds."

Also ruthless, she thought. Roadrunners were one of the few animals that could go head to head with a rattlesnake and prevail. She'd watched this in a video once. The roadrunner had walked right up to the rattlesnake, no fear. The animals had gone back and forth nipping at each other. Blood had spotted the roadrunner's leg. But the roadrunner didn't give a shit. He (or she?) eventually grabbed hold of the snake's head, bashed it against the earth three times, and then devoured the snake whole. The video clip had ended with the snake's rattle hanging out of the roadrunner's mouth like a strange tongue.

Phyllis noted that Deena's yard looked nice since Jeff had uprooted a couple of shrubs. "It's less crowded," Phyllis said.

Deena agreed with Phyllis, but she prickled at the woman feeling at ease expressing her judgment of their yard, which right now had quite a few weeds. Normally, Deena would have gone out and pulled them by now, but she didn't have the strength.

Phyllis shared that a landscaper was coming soon to take out their mesquite tree. "The pods are too much work for me. I can't keep up with them."

Phyllis's husband, Lee, could hardly walk anymore. Deena didn't know much about it, only that for several months now Phyllis has been driving around with a wheelchair lift on the back of her SUV. Deena didn't feel she knew her neighbors well enough to ask questions about their health. Or maybe she just didn't want to hear the answers. Deena hadn't even asked questions when her supervisor at work had taken a couple weeks off for brain surgery. She'd just said to her after she returned, "Welcome back."

Even when Phyllis and Lee had first moved in about two years earlier, Lee hadn't been in great shape. When Deena had introduced herself to them, he'd started to put out his hand, but Phyllis had quickly yelled, "Don't shake his hand! He has shingles!" He'd pulled his hand back. "Oops," he'd said. "Close one."

Since that introduction, Deena had never seen him outside the house other than in the window of the SUV. In contrast, Phyllis was outside every morning and afternoon watering something and, from late summer through the fall, picking up mesquite pods.

The mesquite tree was a scapegoat, Deena thought. Phyllis seemed cheerful enough, but her decision to uproot the mesquite tree seemed to Deena like a small bulbous top of a root vegetable that showed at the soil surface, portending something more hidden beneath. Deena knew this: the thought of Jeff being incapacitated horrified her. She pictured him as a nearly two-hundred-pound infant slurping the marrow out of her bones.

Now Phyllis said, "Good mother. Breastfeeding that baby."

Deena looked down to check that she hadn't inadvertently left a breast exposed, but no, her breasts were properly tucked away. She looked across the street for the roadrunner. It was standing so still that it looked like a yard decoration.

*

Deena's friend, Hazel, was always conducting experiments with the men she dated. Like when she'd dated Gerald, the guy who brewed beer in his kitchen and couldn't shut up about his chocolate coffee brew, Hazel had once simulated giving a blowjob to an empty bottle of beer while Gerald was on the phone with his mother. The question prompting the experiment: was Gerald sexually repressed? The conclusion: yes. Evidence:

the mean faces he made at her during the phone call and what he said after about how she'd disrespected his mother. Real-world application of the results of her research: she promptly broke up with him.

Deena decided she would conduct an experiment of her own: if Jeff came home to find her passed out to the point that not even their baby's cries could wake her, would he finally step it up a little? Make a more concerted effort to help her get the rest she so desperately needs?

Hazel said, "I don't think this is such a good idea. What are you going to do if you don't like the results of the experiment? Have you thought about that?"

"You seem rather certain Jeff will fail," Deena said.

"It's the poor experimental design I take issue with," Hazel said. "Being conked out on Ambien and wine seems as good as leaving the baby home alone."

But wasn't prioritizing her own rest the correct thing to do? The way that making the baby sleep in a crib was the correct thing to do, according to the pediatrician, even though intuitively it felt wrong.

Deena had expected her friend to laugh devilishly on the other end of the phone, to give pointers.

"Whose side are you on?" Deena said.

"The baby's?" Hazel said.

Deena sighed. Disturbed by the movement, the baby opened his eyes briefly, but soon closed them again. They were still out on the porch, the baby having lasted nearly forty minutes before passing out again.

Hazel said, "What if Jeff comes home late? What if he doesn't come home at all?"

"The pediatrician said the safest place for the baby is a crib," Deena said.

Hazel was silent for a while. Deena felt that Hazel was considering her the way one might a pot of hot soup that needed to be transferred to a storage container: considering whether energy and time saved was worth the risk of lifting the heavy pot and pouring instead of taking the slower, more cautious route of using a ladle.

Deena said, "The baby won't die from a little interruption to his non-stop feeding frenzy."

"You're exhausted. Your logic is out of tune. You're like a wonky guitar," Hazel said.

"Hence the Ambien," Deena said.

"I could come over and help," Hazel said. She didn't sound particularly enthusiastic, though.

"That would tarnish the experiment," Deena said.

"You already knew Jeff was the lovee in the relationship," Hazel said then.

"The what?" Deena said.

"In every relationship, one person doles out more love than the other. That person is the lover. The other is the lovee. I don't mean Jeff doesn't love you, of course. But he's not exactly a relationship nurturer. You know that. You've always known that."

Deena pictured Phyllis picking up pods and driving around that wheelchair lift.

"I don't want to be the lover," she said.

"It's not a bad thing," Hazel said.

"Which are you?" Deena asked.

"It's not a hard and fast rule. It can depend on the pairing. But lovee, almost always."

"Fuck this shit," Deena said.

"Except with Nigel," Hazel said. "I would have had a dozen babies with that man."

"Giving birth is evidence that I'm the lover?"

"Well, giving birth voluntarily," Hazel said, "Yes."

*

There was a man Deena looked out for every day at about 9:00 am and later at about a quarter to four, pushing a baby stroller. The man dressed like Deena did these days, in wrinkled and/ or stained T-shirts. His beard seemed to get more unruly by the day. The predictability of his schedule combined with the slovenliness of his appearance meant, she was fairly certain, that he was at home with his baby all day long, like Deena. She imagined he cared for the baby while the mother was at an office, like Jeff. She imagined other things, too, like that he danced with his baby the way that Deena danced with her baby, twirling the baby around her living room to the dark, smoky music of Tom Waits. And that he sat on his porch with his baby and pointed out flora and fauna.

She'd constructed a fantasy involving this man. In it, one morning (or afternoon, either one) the man pushes the baby stroller up Deena's driveway and to her porch. He doesn't say a word, just joins her on the porch with his baby. They sit there a while, the sun making them all incredibly sleepy. Then he takes her hand, and they go inside the house. He places the babies together in the crib, kisses their heads, a magic spell that makes the babies sleep for hours. Then he takes Deena's hand, leads her to the bed and cuddles with her, and casts the same sleep spell on her head. They sleep and sleep and sleep, and she is so grateful, she thinks she would do anything for this man.

It's Sleeping Beauty in reverse. Funny, because Deena had always hated how passive women are in so many fairy tales, Sleeping Beauty worst of all because the princess does absolutely nothing but sleep throughout nearly the entire tale. And that was just the clean Disney version. In an older version of the story, the sleeping beauty is raped in her sleep by a married king and carries to term twin babies, even giving birth to them without waking. "Bullshit," she'd said when Hazel told her that some years ago. Now that she'd experienced birth herself, Deena found the tale even more ridiculous.

*

When, predictably, the guy who pushed the stroller appeared a few minutes before four that afternoon, not long after Deena got off the phone with Hazel, Deena tried to casually but pointedly look at him so as to catch his eye. When that didn't work, she called out, "Good afternoon!" He startled. When he saw her, he just put his hand up briefly in answer. Then he looked straight ahead again. It seemed to her he pushed the stroller a little faster.

The man's slovenliness was what made him attractive to her. Deena saw his appearance as indication of his mutual suffering. It made him endearing. But she understood that her own slovenliness had the opposite effect. She was undesirable, a woman to be avoided. Even if she were to offer, say, a blowjob in return for several hours of uninterrupted sleep, she doubted there was a man, other than a scurvy creep with whom she wouldn't dare leave her baby, who would take her up on the offer in her current state.

She thought of Shannon Rourke, a woman she'd gone to college with, who now had five kids, was a Ph.D. student, and who boasted on her blog about how she read a minimum of three books a week, mopped the kitchen twice a day, made her own cleaning products and deodorant, and was at work on a novel and a memoir both on top of her dissertation. Is that what it took to earn some damn sleep? You had to be a fucking superhero during your waking hours?

Phyllis came back outside. She waved to Deena.

"Yes?" Deena said, half afraid Phyllis was about to offer some further judgment about her mothering.

"You're not going anywhere, are you?" Phyllis said.

The roadrunner was back, this time a few houses down, standing in the shadows of a palo verde trunk. Deena thought of the roadrunner and coyote cartoons, how no matter what Wile E. Coyote tried—dynamite, a wrecking ball, a boxing glove attached to a spring—the plan failed him. He was fated to fail, and the cruelest part was that every time he died, he was resurrected so that he could live out the same damn story again. And again and again ad infinitum. That must be what hell is, Deena remembered thinking as a kid—not so much the failure part as the repetition, the monotony.

She said to Phyllis, "I'm not going anywhere for at least two and a half months."

Phyllis asked if Deena would keep her eye out for a package that was supposed to be delivered that day. "We'll be gone for only about forty minutes, but of course it will probably be delivered the minute I leave. It's really important, and I worry about someone stealing it, you know?"

Deena didn't know, but she agreed to watch for the package. Then she watched Phyllis's SUV back out of the garage. From the passenger seat, Lee looked straight ahead, seemingly oblivious to Deena watching him. Then they were gone.

Just as Phyllis had predicted, a UPS truck pulled up in between their houses about five minutes after Phyllis and Lee drove away. That damn UPS truck pulled up in between their houses nearly every single day, but always his deliveries were for Phyllis and Lee.

Deena hoped, as she had every day for the last few weeks, that today the UPS guy would have a package for her, too. Even after he walked up Phyllis's driveway with a box so large she could probably curl herself up inside it, then returned to the truck empty-handed, Deena held out hope that there was something in that Santa bag for her.

She'd received zero packages since giving birth. Not even flowers from her employer, whom she knew had sent flowers to coworkers when they'd had babies because she'd seen the thank-you notes pinned to the corkboard in the office breakroom. An oversight, Hazel claimed. "You know how disorganized your company is."

Before Deena had given birth, there'd been plenty of gifts, albeit for the baby. Onesies, hand-knitted booties, pastel blankets mysteriously labeled "receiving blankets." Deena had pictured people holding these blankets out like baskets in church, in which she was to place the baby like a ten-dollar bill. The only gift that had really been for Deena had been a bottle of whiskey and that had been from Hazel. Now that the baby was no longer inside her, Deena felt like discarded wrapping paper at a birthday party.

The UPS guy climbed back into the truck, his only delivery for Deena a head nod.

She felt like hurling something, only the thing strapped to her chest was not a stone or a stick of TNT, it was her baby, and he wasn't to blame for her giftlessness. Or, as many people would point out, he was her damn gift. A treasure. A miracle. What more did she want?

Well, chicken parmesan, for starters.

Deena need not retrieve Phyllis's package as long as she remained on the porch to monitor the situation, but after several minutes of wondering what the hell was in that huge package—a television, a wine fridge—her curiosity got the best of her. She could peek inside, then re-tape the box. It's not like

Phyllis would accuse her of opening the package for which she'd asked Deena to keep an eye out.

So she stood up ever so slowly so as not to wake the baby inside its detachable uterus, and she gathered scissors and packaging tape from her kitchen and stuffed these things into the smaller of her two diaper bags, this one intended to look like a fashionable purse. A shower gift from a ditzy cousin. She looked about the street to see if anyone was around. Then she crossed the invisible divide between her yard and Phyllis's.

*

The box was not the first thing that caught Deena's attention when she came face to face with Phyllis's front door; it was the key in the lock. A dull, copper-colored key seemingly identical to the key Deena carried around on her keyring.

She'd seen the inside of this house before, but not since Phyllis and Lee had occupied it. They were the third couple to live in the house since Deena and Jeff had moved in. The previous couples had both been young. Even so, visiting this house back then, Deena had been struck by how different her adult decorating aesthetic was from her slightly younger neighbors. In the hands of both the previous couples, the house had reminded Deena of the homes of her aunts and uncles when she was a kid. Clean, uncluttered, yes, but also sterile and fake, like a department store display. Take the big glass bowl of decorative balls made of silver wire that Brie and John, the first couple, had placed on the console table. Or the mass-produced signs hung about by Leanne and Marcus, signs that read "Love," "Family," "Joy," and "Hope." Deena had joked to Jeff after that they ought to put up word signs of their own—"Hate," "Greed," "Corpses," "Decapitation"—then invite Leanne and Marcus over for dinner just to see the looks on their faces.

The doorknob turned with the same stiffness as Deena's own front door. When she pushed open the door, the first thing she noticed was the smell—acidic and sweet, but a little off, like a moldy lemon. Shannon Rourke had written an entire blog post once about uses for a moldy lemon, a list that had included making your own penicillin.

Deena quickly saw that the house was no longer reminiscent of a department store display. The house, in fact, made Deena's house seem tidy, in contrast, even though neither she nor Jeff had yet to put away the pantry items he'd brought home several days earlier—spaghetti, oatmeal, cans of beans, etc. Cardboard boxes were stacked about the foyer—many of them empty. The boxes that weren't empty contained items such as a 40-pack bag of adult diapers, a 24-roll pack of toilet paper, a handicap toilet seat.

Moving further into the house, Deena saw that one of the recliners in their living area was littered with crumbs, like a child's car seat. Next to the recliner on the floor was a donut-shaped pillow in a red tartan plaid print.

Even the walls and the curtain covering the sliding glass door were sad in their matching taupe, the color of a stick of concealer.

Phyllis had made a small effort to make the house nice by placing a vase of flowers on the bar, but within the surrounding environment the gladiolas seemed to Deena like a small, injured fawn in a nature video, a fawn that had gotten abandoned by its group. It was only a matter of time before something, whether a predator or simply the harshness of the elements, ravaged the animal.

Deena realized she no longer envied Phyllis the box on her porch, nor was she curious to see what was inside. No, Phyllis was not someone to be envied. Phyllis was, in fact, a tragic character, like Wile E. Coyote, for whom the normal laws of nature didn't apply. This had perhaps been most clearly illustrated when he placed a painting of a continuous cliff road to conceal that the real road ended, crumbled into an abyss. Fantastically, the roadrunner enters the painting, runs on untarnished. As if that weren't impossible enough, as the roadrunner disappears in the distance, a huge semi comes roaring out of the painting. Yet when Wile E. Coyote tries to enter the painting himself, he rips through the canvas, plummets to another death.

This is what Deena was thinking when she spotted the box of chocolates next to the coffee maker. She opened the box to survey what was inside. Meatball-sized truffles that smelled of cinnamon. She started to reach for one and then stopped herself. The chocolates belonged to Phyllis, and the woman deserved whatever small pleasure she could rake up from life.

But then Deena pictured Jeff sitting in the Italian restaurant with a drink, waiting on the food he ordered in the restaurant rather than on the phone so that he could have a reason to order that drink and then another. By the time the food was ready, he'd be tipsy enough to not care if the food got cold while he had a third drink.

She decided she deserved a truffle as much as Phyllis did and that taking just one truffle wasn't so terrible. Maybe Phyllis wouldn't even remember how many she'd already eaten, the way that Deena had been confused that afternoon when she went to the kitchen for another piece of zucchini bread only to find that the bread was gone, its crumpled foil wrapper in the wastebasket.

But Deena didn't stop at one truffle. She ate a second and a third. When the roadrunner appeared on the wall outside Phyllis's kitchen window, the wall that separated their two yards, Deena thought of the little girl on that television show who had taken the cake, literally. Before the researcher left her alone in the room with the slice of pink-frosted cake, he had shown her a dolly and said to her, "Would you like to have this dolly?" The girl had smiled and nodded. The researcher had said that if the girl could resist eating the cake for fifteen minutes, then she could have the dolly and the cake both. "Does that sound good?" he'd said. "Can you do that?" The girl had nodded.

The researcher wasn't even gone for thirty seconds when the girl dipped her pinky finger into the cake's frosting. A few seconds later, she pinched crumbs from the cake. Then she grabbed fistfuls of the cake and shoved them into her mouth, one after another, until there was nothing left but a pink smear on the white plate.

Deena had thought at the time that the girl must have imagined she could get away with it somehow, claim that the cake just disappeared, that she had nothing to do with it. That the girl believed the researcher would not possibly deny her the dolly. But now, as Deena placed a fourth truffle into her mouth, she concluded that no, the girl had been smarter than that. The girl had understood that life didn't play out the way you were told it would. She'd understood that you better take what you could while you had the chance.

THE PREGNANCY GAME

At Gwen's insistence, we're in the woods behind her house. Pine trees like thick arrows point toward the bleached sky. Beneath our feet, copper-colored needles. The air smells of sap and soil and the stagnant water of the bayou that we can't see from here but is always near. It's a Saturday in late September, the fall of our seventh-grade year.

Gwen has created a game board on the forest floor by making a trail of the pink paper plates purchased for her older sister Patrice's baby shower, a baby shower that never took place. We were all at Gwen's house when her mother got off the phone with Patrice two weeks ago. "Your sister lost the baby": those were Gwen's mother's words. Minh and Tahlia don't know what Gwen and I later learned—that Patrice is still carrying that dead baby inside her.

Gwen says that Minh, Tahlia, and I will be the pawns.

Along with the paper plates, Gwen has brought the fuzzy, white die she won in a claw machine at the arcade. A game turn consists of a player rolling that die, then walking the designated number of plates from start, picking up the plate where she lands and turning it over to read what it says.

Gwen must have spent hours writing on these plates, planning out the rules. That's typical Gwen. Years ago, the first time she spent the night at my house, my mom went on about how precise Gwen was. "Whoever heard of a little girl measuring out the amount of toothpaste on her brush like that? And did you see how long she chewed between each bite of spaghetti?" she said to my dad. "She counts to forty," I said. "Good lord," my mom said.

I feel slightly hurt to learn about this game at the same time as Minh and Tahlia. I'm her best friend, after all. But she's been distant since we learned about Patrice's baby. I think of how one of the magicians in last spring's Magic Showcase, a goofy looking guy in a big, curly-haired wig, held a sheet up in front of a woman and then pulled the sheet back to reveal nothing but air. Of course, the woman couldn't have gone far because he made her reappear a few seconds later, but though I knew she was there somewhere, I couldn't see her.

Gwen points to Minh and me and says, "You're both pregnant." To Tahlia, she says, "You're not pregnant."

"Yes!" Tahlia says. "And you?" she says to Gwen, who stands apart from us, like she is a cue stick and we are racked balls.

Gwen cracks her neck. "I'm the Right to Life Activist. Kind of like the robber in Settlers of Catan."

"What do you steal? Our babies?" Minh says, picking dirt from underneath her nails.

"Fetuses, technically," Gwen says. "They're not born yet. But no. What I steal is everything but the fetus."

I feel myself shiver even though it's humid out, the temperature still in the nineties.

Gwen says that because Tahlia isn't pregnant, she gets to go first.

"Why?" Minh asks.

"Because it's the rule. Pregnant pawns always go last," Gwen says.

"Not in the real world. What about those expectant mothers parking spots?" Minh says.

Gwen rolls her eyes. "Seriously? You think that's a perk worth getting excited about?" She looks to Tahlia and tells her to roll the fuzzy die.

The die rolls over the pine needles and stops when it bumps against a cone. Five.

Before Tahlia picks up the plate, Gwen explains that there are two messages beneath each plate: one for pregnant pawns, one for unpregnant pawns. Tahlia should read the one for unpregnant pawns.

Tahlia reads her pink paper plate aloud. "You're a slut who had casual sex and then took a morning-after pill. Go back to start."

Tahlia laughs, flips her hair. "Hey, I'll take slut over having babies any day." She walks back to the start plate, rejoining the rest of us.

Minh says, "Is she back at start because she had casual sex? Or because she took a morning-after pill?"

Gwen just stares at Minh.

"Both," I say. "Right?"

Gwen gives me a pinprick of a smile.

Minh is next. She rolls a six. The paper plate reads, "You ended up pregnant as a result of being raped. You got an abortion. But in your state, it's illegal to get abortions in rape cases. In fact, your rapist can sue you for doing so, and that's just what he's done. Go back to start."

Minh says, "How is that even a thing? A rapist suing his victim?"

"It's a thing all right," Gwen says.

"Well, what if I lived in a state where it's legal to have an abortion in the case of rape? Would I get to go forward then?"

Gwen looks to me. "Frances?"

Though I can't see the horizon beyond all these trees, I know the sun is starting to set because I spot a mosquito on my thigh, its long legs reminding me of the stitches in Gwen's forehead when she fell off her bike a few years ago. She didn't cry a single tear. Instead, she punched the asphalt, injuring herself further.

I flick the mosquito away, worry about blood diseases. I say, "I don't think moving forward is the objective of this game."

Gwen nods her head in approval.

"What is the objective then?" Minh says. "To further overpopulate the planet? To turn women into baby-incubator automatons?"

A mosquito lands on Gwen's arm and she smacks it dead. Rubs the residue onto her denim shorts. She ignores Minh, says, "Frances, it's your turn."

I reluctantly retrieve the fuzzy die, which is slightly damp and more brown than white now. When I release it, the die rolls into Gwen's pristine white sneaker and stops. Three. I walk slowly to the third paper plate and pick it up. I stare at it.

"Read what it says." Gwen smacks another mosquito, this time on her neck. Again, she wipes the residue onto her shorts.

I read, "Your fetus is not viable, but it's post 20 weeks." I stop.

"Read," Gwen says again.

I suck in my breath. "So you must continue to carry the pregnancy even though there's no chance the baby will survive after birth. Move forward six spaces and read the next plate."

I look to Gwen, my best friend since we were five. Her face is stone, but I can see through to the jagged mineral deposits, the hollow cavity inside.

I don't move.

"Forward six," Gwen says.

"Gwen," I say.

"You can't quit," Gwen says. "No quitters."

Still, I stand there. Minh and Tahlia look back and forth between Gwen and me. Somewhere a police siren sharpens then dulls. Dogs bark.

Gwen walks over to me, says, "I'll go for you then."

Before I can say anything, Gwen raises her hand. Smacks my cheek.

Minh says, "What the fuck?"

I grit my teeth so as not to cry.

Gwen holds open her hand to show me the mosquito bits and the blood. My blood. I wait for her to wipe it onto my shorts, since it's my blood, my dead mosquito, but she doesn't. She wipes the mess onto her own shorts. She moves forward.

THE DIFFERENCE BETWEEN ME AND EVERYONE ELSE

I'm refilling my plastic cup with ginger ale in the hostess's kitchen when a woman, the mother of the naked toddler with the obscenely long penis, says to another woman, "I've been in three fatal car accidents."

She could have stepped out of a Dorothea Lange photograph: both hardy and soft at once. I'll call her Biscuit.

The second woman says, "What do you mean fatal?" She's more like an opera cake, intricate and linear.

Biscuit says, "Lethal. Deadly." With her free hand, she makes a slicing motion across the front of her throat.

Opera Cake says, "Your fault?"

I almost knock over a bottle of Malbec as I set the ginger ale back onto the counter. I catch the bottle just in time.

Opera Cake says, "A spilled bottle of wine is a criminal act where I come from."

I laugh nervously. The bottle is still in my hand, and I want to put it to my lips. Just a taste: what my toddler, Jack, says of every dessert within a ten-foot radius. He can sniff out sugar as well as a bloodhound tracks the scent of rotting flesh. It's innate in humans, this sensitivity to sugar. I fall asleep on the floor of Jack's bedroom on the mornings he wakes before 5:00 am and I wake again later to find him burrowed like a rodent beneath my shirt, binging on breastmilk. That's me with liquor, though. Before I went all-in on alcohol, I once tracked cannoli and eclairs. When my friend Jeannie and I traveled Europe by train in college, we made it a point to sample at least one pastry (and at least one boy) in every city we visited.

But since the DUI and my court-mandated AA, I'm drinking ginger ale.

Biscuit says, "No, not my fault. The first time was when I was a kid. Some maniac was driving the wrong way on the highway at night. My dad swerved just enough that we got side-swiped, but the other guy crashed into the median at like 90 miles an hour. His car contracted like a Slinky."

Opera Cake says, "Whoa."

Biscuit's naked toddler enters the kitchen then and asks for more apple juice.

Biscuit says, "You're cut off."

I try not to stare at his penis, which dangles like Opera Cake's oversized earrings as she laughs.

"Juice," he repeats.

"Water," Biscuit says.

He drops the empty cup on the tile and stomps out of the kitchen.

"I did that once when Will said I'd had enough wine," Opera Cake says. "This was at his mother's house. I mean, is there such a thing as enough wine in that circumstance? The glass was hand-painted. Colorful shards all over the kitchen, like the entrails of a piñata. Of course, he covered for me. Didn't want his mom thinking he'd married a raging alcoholic."

She and Biscuit laugh.

I don't make a sound.

My friend Jeannie says it could have happened to anybody, that the state's no-tolerance DUI law is ridiculous. "I mean a 0.05 blood alcohol level? That's like a single drink. You weren't drunk. You didn't hurt anyone. Jack wasn't in the car. Who hasn't driven after having a drink or two?" But Jeannie doesn't have a kid. She and I got drunk on margaritas one night when Jack was about five months old, and he cried when I handed him a bottle of untainted breastmilk from the fridge. Kept grabbing at my chest. I cried, too. Jeannie didn't understand why I was upset.

Biscuit picks up the cup and puts it in the sink. "I actually sort of like my mother-in-law, but only for about an hour at a time."

I consider pouring out the ginger ale and filling my cup with Malbec. Biscuit and Opera Cake are both drinking wine, and one glass is not a big deal as long as I wash it down with water before leaving the party. But then I think of Jack playing in the kiddie pool out back in his clothes. He's modest, even in front of his grandparents. Although his modesty can't possibly have anything to do with his penis, not at his age, I worry about his penis. It's stubby like a pencil eraser. Maybe it's normal, or maybe I did that to him, drinking all that chocolate soy milk when I was pregnant. I was so proud of myself for not drinking more than a few sips of alcohol for nine whole months. I didn't learn until my last month of pregnancy that soy mimics estrogen, that it can decrease the size of male sexual organs in utero. Scientists are constantly discovering new mistakes it's too late to undo.

Biscuit says, "So fatal accident number two happened when I was in high school. I left a party at like one a.m. with some guy I'd just met, to go buy donuts." She looks back and forth at both me and Opera Cake. "One minute he's driving. The next we're on the side of the road, and I see that a tree limb has punctured the windshield and punched through the guy's skull like a fist."

"Oh my god," Opera Cake says. "How did he crash?"

"I don't know," Biscuit says. "I blacked out."

Opera Cake says, "Remind me to never get into a car with you."

Biscuit shrugs. "I don't believe in curses."

Jack enters the kitchen then. His clothes are soaked. He's dripping on the floor. "Mama, I'm cold," he says.

Biscuit is quick. Before I can think to put my ginger ale down, she's opened a drawer and has wrapped my child's shoulders in a red kitchen towel. He looks like he may fall asleep standing.

She says, "We need to get you out of those wet clothes." She tugs at his shirt.

"I've got it," I say.

Biscuit looks slightly startled. Then she smiles. "Sorry," she says. "I go into mother mode, you know?"

"Sure," I say quietly.

"Come here, Jack," I say, and he seems to look at me for a long second, as though he's reluctant to leave Biscuit's more capable hands.

I lead Jack to the bathroom, where I undress him and towel him off with a clean bath towel from the hostess's linen closet. The smell of his skin reminds me of the aftermath of rainstorms when I was a kid. I spent hours collecting the animals that surfaced after heavy rains—frogs and crawdads and worms. Once: a baby bird whose nest fell to the earth. My mother said the bird's wing was broken. Then she said that because I'd handled the bird, the mother wouldn't come back for it. I thought I'd rescued the animal, but it turned out that my human scent, something I couldn't smell, had as good as marked the bird for death.

Years later, when I told my friend Jeannie that story, she said, "That's a myth. Your scent didn't kill that bird. The parents abandoned it because they knew there was nothing they could do to save it."

I wrap Jack in the towel like a burrito. When I return to the kitchen, Jack in my arms, Opera Cake is saying, "Oh my god. Oh my god." She throws her hand up over her mouth.

On the drive home, I eye my sleeping child through the rearview mirror, his head slumped against his shoulder at what seems like an impossible angle, and I shiver. Whatever story

Biscuit told, I think it can't be as bad as the terrible things I imagine.

Jeannie says the difference between me and everyone else is that I got caught, but there's so much Jeannie doesn't know. Like that time she and I got drunk on margaritas on my back porch, Jack developed a severe diaper rash because I spent the next morning vomiting into the toilet while my baby cried and cried from his crib. Like how once I bought wine from the grocery store on the way to pick up Jack from daycare after work. It was a two-serving carton, and I barely drank a quarter of it before retrieving him from the nursery floor, where he was flipping through a board book of smiling human faces. But that evening while he nursed, he studied me intently, as he always did when he nursed, and I thought about something I'd read: how newborns can distinguish their mother's milk from other mothers' milk by scent alone. I wondered what chemical markers Jack could smell on me. That he could taste. I don't mean the wine exactly. I mean how an animal knows an odor is human.

GALACTAGOGUES

The voices of the new mothers gathered in the lobby carry
to the examination room, where Carla waits for the midwife.
Accompanied by the cries of their infants, the mothers in the
mom-and-baby group talk mostly about breastfeeding—the
tingling, often painful, sensation of letdown; the nuances of
their infants' suckles; breast milk's sweet, earthy odor. One
woman, whose high-pitched voice Carla recognizes from her
prenatal care centering group—her name is Amanda—admits
to tasting her own milk. She unhelpfully describes her milk
as both tangy and mild. Carla, a high school English teacher,
gives the description a D. What does that even mean, tangy
and mild? Amanda is the same woman who shared once at
centering group that she dreamt she'd breastfed her cats.
When a well-meaning but stupid aunt recently suggested
Carla and Lowell get a cat, Carla imagined a gray cat kneading

her breast to make the milk come, its scratchy tongue lapping at her areolas.

It was in this exam room that a nurse had checked the dilation of Carla's cervix before approving her admittance into one of the birthing rooms. How pleased she had been to claim the large room with the Jacuzzi. Between contractions on the drive over, she'd chanted, "Jacuzzi room, Jacuzzi room, Jacuzzi room," much to Lowell's chagrin. He'd said, "Aren't there more important things to concentrate on right now than a Jacuzzi?" After bracing herself against the glove compartment during a contraction, she repeated, "Jacuzzi room."

Six weeks and two days have passed since that night. She doesn't want to be here, but the alternative for the standard six-week post-partum checkup was a home visit, and there is too much she doesn't want people to see: Lowell's makeshift bed on the sofa, the milk that now dominates their freezer because she cannot let it dry up.

The mothers in the lobby talk about "galactagogues," a word that conjures space explorers for Carla, but really "galacto" means milk or milky; "galaxy" is a derivative. Galactagogues are foods that stimulate or increase milk production. One woman says she thinks that's nonsense, and Amanda quickly retorts, "Oh, it's definitely true. After I've had a bowl of oatmeal, the milk will spray ten feet out if I let it. I'm like one of those high-powered showerheads."

Now that Carla is here in the building where she labored, she can't stop herself from tiptoeing around the corner past the kitchenette to the room where she gave birth. The shade is drawn up. An ocotillo outside has sprouted fiery red tips like stretched nipples.

Strangers don't know this about her: that she labored and gave birth like any other mother. The proof is hidden, not on display in a stroller or strapped to her torso where people can see. But her uterus knows, even though the books say it will have shrunken to its original size (a standard shot glass) by now. Her bladder knows. Her stitched perineum. Her breasts.

Well before her due date, Carla met with one of the midwives to review her birth plan, a homework assignment in which she was supposed to envision how she wanted the birth process to unfold, from whether she wanted music playing while she labored (and what kind) to whether she wanted the baby handed to her immediately or sponged off first, like a nugget of gold panned in a muddy river basin. Carla turned in a ten-paged double-spaced typed document, and the midwife said, "Why don't you just summarize it for me?" When Carla was done, the first thing the midwife said was, "You know you can't control the birth process, right? Believe me, there's no control in birth."

Carla had wanted to say, then why did you ask me to write up a birth plan? A plan is a map, a blueprint, a procedure. But instead she said, "Of course. I understand."

And she went home and revised the birth plan to sound less controlling, even though no one would see it other than her. Lowell said, "Just tell me what you want from me, and I'll do my best."

On the bed now is a plate of half-eaten crackers, wrapped cheeses, and grapes. Beside the plate is a plastic baby doll wearing an old-fashioned cloth diaper held together by safety pins. The doll's little mouth is open, poised to nurse. The remains of a lactation consultation perhaps.

In the lobby of the birth center, Amanda declares proudly that her baby has gained a pound a week since birth.

"That's some milk you have, lady," another woman says.

What follows is a burst of laughter that sounds to Carla like flatulence.

She sits on the bed. She pulls a grape from its stem. It's cool in her mouth. She unwraps a cheese and spoons it onto a cracker. It's creamy and delicious despite being processed. Always Carla is hungry. Because always Millie is hungry. Millie of the ether. Galactic Millie. She may be returning to dust, but she still wants.

Carla has long loved the process of revision, the way something scrappy and ugly can be transformed into something exquisite. She loves the labor of it, so much, in fact, that if the words seem to come too easily, too quickly, she's suspicious of them. She tells her students that if an essay they submit contains more than 30 percent of the words of the original draft than they have probably not done that essay justice in revision.

She'd thought of motherhood as a process of revision: the way her body was remade day by day, hour by hour, all those months; the way her identity was remade. For instance, people who had before ignored her at best, at other times cut her in line at the grocery or complained to the HOA about a few weeds in her yard, smiled approvingly at her once it was evident that she was more than just Carla Woods. She felt that shift internally, too. She ate more vegetables, went to bed early, bought a stuffed bunny at a store where she would have before shopped for a new pair of jeans.

What she hadn't considered, certainly not after she was well past the thirteen-week marker, the possibility of doom safely behind her (or so she'd thought), is that her narrative of motherhood could be susceptible to revision, too.

Like that woman in the news who had the pet alligator she babied. The old Carla would have pitied the woman. She would have called her a nut.

But now Carla eyes the doll next to her on the bed with longing. The doll cannot replace Millie, of course, but if Carla were to close her eyes and pretend, would the doll feel so different?

She brushes the doll's arm as if by accident. When the doll does not recoil, she touches its cheek.

"Hi," Carla whispers.

Amanda yelps from the lobby. "He's got the most powerful latch-on of any baby in the universe, I tell you. Sometimes I think he's going to take my nipple clean off."

To latch on, Carla thinks, can mean to close or fasten, to hold onto, to attach oneself to, to join with, to take possession of.

Carla takes the doll into her arms and sinks back against the quilted pillow.

She'd held her daughter for several hours before the nurse took her away. She did not want to mourn a faceless child—a mere pattern of kicks at five in the morning, fierce bones that prodded the thick muscle of her uterus.

Even so, if it weren't for the photographs, Carla knows she would not be able to picture Millie's face now. She has never been good at recalling visual details.

But Carla refuses to say she "lost" the baby. Millie is not misplaced. Besides, given the process of birth, every baby is a loss—a removal, a lessening, an injury.

"Are you hungry?" she asks the doll in her arms.

She nursed Millie after everyone but Lowell left the room. He didn't say anything, but she'd understood it made him uncomfortable, her milk, or colostrum really, yellow and thick, on their child's unmoving lips, making her and Millie's skin sticky. And the fact that she'd pinched and pulled at her nipple to get the colostrum to emerge. She'd read about how to do this, known that many newborns did not latch on immediately. She'd been prepared for this, at least.

Carla holds the doll to her chest. She feels the prickling like tiny cactus spines prodding her milk ducts. Soon, oxytocin makes her tipsy, and her animosity toward Amanda is like a bouillon cube dissolved, watery now, cloudy. Like the hazy dust that makes up so much of the universe. She thinks that she and the other mothers are like stars, the way their bodies are always burning, burning, burning. Recycling particles so that new stars can form.

So, when Amanda says, "It's all so wild. I mean their flesh is our flesh. Or was. And our flesh was theirs and is theirs and keeps on becoming theirs," Carla nods and says in response, "And every day they claim more of us."

A MOUTH IS A HOUSE FOR TEETH

The mother is never to answer the door. If there's a knock, she is to hide. She is to hide herself and the girl and make it appear that no one is home. Unless the knock is the husband's secret knock that only the two of them know. Then she is to open the door. There's a keyhole, of course, but the husband doesn't take the key with him when he's away. For starters, carrying a key is a nuisance. Second, why does he need a key if she is always home? Third, and most important, what if someone who wishes to hurt the girl and the mother steals the key from the husband and lets himself into the house?

The outside is dangerous to the girl, and by proxy, dangerous to the mother. In truth, the outside would be dangerous to the mother even if she were not a mother, but because there is the child, the mother is particularly vulnerable.

The only time she should ever open the door other than when she hears the secret knock that only she and the husband know is when there is a supply drop. She knows supplies have arrived because she hears the supply box thunk the concrete. She knows the thunk is the supply box because she schedules the delivery of the supply boxes, and always the boxes show up at the exact second they are scheduled.

Now, for instance. She hears the scheduled thunk. She looks through the peephole and sees the box, its dimensions distorted by the peephole's fisheye lens. She opens the door. There before her is the box.

There before her is also a decapitated head of a rabbit, a few inches from the box. It's shriveled, old. Through the peephole, she assumed it was a rock that had gotten kicked up by wind. Actually, perhaps the truth is she didn't think anything of it at all.

Now, the dead rabbit's dull black eyes seem to stare at her feet. She looks around, but she sees no one, not even the drone that delivered the box, not even her closest neighbor, who is not a mother of a young child, and who, therefore, is free to go outside as she pleases. What the mother does see is the street, the street that goes for miles and miles and that connects to other streets that go for miles and miles, all of which connect to the interstate system, like a capillary in a network of blood vessels that circuit the country. Follow it, and you can go anywhere. She feels the pull of the street. Or maybe this pull is just hormones. She knows better than to trust hormones. Hormones are how she got here in the first place.

She drags the supply box into the house and quickly closes and locks the door. She looks through the peephole at the rabbit head that looks like a stone. The mother doesn't hear the girl approach. The girl says, "Daddy home?" and the mother screams.

When the girl cries, the mother hugs her. "Sorry, I didn't know you were there. It's just the supply box. See?"

"When is Daddy coming home?" the girl asks.

"Like I've told you, Baby. I don't know."

"When's he going to call?"

"I don't know. Let's see about breakfast, OK?"

The girl returns to her bedroom, shuts the door.

The mother looks out the peephole again. The rabbit head is gone.

She puts her hand on the knob, thinks of opening the door to be sure the rabbit head wasn't just blown closer to the door where the fisheye can't reach. But to open the door again, when she has already dragged in the supply box, would be breaking protocol.

As long as they follow protocol, they are safe. The girl is safe. The mother is safe. The husband has told her this hundreds of times.

She takes her hand off the door.

*

When the husband is away, there is no certainty of when he will return. There is no certainty he will return at all. This is basic common sense and would be so even if the husband's work wasn't dangerous, which it is. It would be common sense even if he could talk openly to the mother and the girl about his work, which he cannot. Sometimes when the husband has had a drink and is feeling good, he might say, like they do in the movies, "I'd tell you, but then I'd have to kill you." Then he laughs. Or he doesn't.

It's been five days now since the husband last called. This is not unusual. When he doesn't call for several days, sometimes the mother imagines the husband is dead. She wonders how much time will pass before someone informs her.

Sometimes when he does call, like he does today when she and the girl are eating blueberry pancakes, and says, "It's been a really tough week" and "Man, am I exhausted," and doesn't ask how she's doing, she wishes he were dead.

When the girl was born, the husband was always finding excuses to leave the house. They needed more diapers. They needed more crackers. The car needed a full detail and wax.

She says, "Before you go, I need to tell you something. There was a rabbit head next to the supply box this morning."

"A what?"

"A decapitated rabbit head," she says.

The girl pays close attention.

The mother continues. "And then, barely a minute later, when I looked out the peephole, the rabbit head was gone."

"Probably a hawk or a cat," the husband says.

"That decapitated it, or that hauled it away as soon as I dragged in the supply box?"

"Both?" he says. "I'm sure it's nothing to worry about. You're following protocol?"

She says, "Of course."

"Then you have nothing to worry about," he says.

"The head was shriveled, old," she says.

"Probably the wind lifted it as easily as a pebble." The husband asks the girl how she's doing.

The girl says, "I had to get an antibiotic. I had an infection in my leg."

The husband, who seconds earlier seemed disinterested in them and in a rush to get off the phone to get dinner, now has a dozen questions. The girl tells him about how she had a cut and the mother left a bandage on her leg for three days, forgetting to change it or check it, and about how when the mother did pull the bandage off, finally, beneath were two large mounds full of pus. Then the next day, there were several more pustules on the girl's leg. Hence the antibiotic delivered in a supply box.

The husband says, "Did you not bathe her for three whole days?"

The mother says, "I forgot. And it's not like she gets dirty never leaving the house. I'm just trying to survive. It's not easy doing everything myself."

He says, "Well, I hope our daughter survives, too."

The mother says nothing.

After they say their goodbyes and hang up the phone, the girl says, "I wish I had gotten to see the rabbit head. I wish you had called me."

"That would be breaking protocol now, wouldn't it?" the mother says.

"I never get to see anything," the girl says.

Of course, the mother longs for the girl to grow up differently. She longs for the girl to be safe in the outside world, to roam free, the way she once had. So long ago now it seemed like a dream. But absolutely she must ensure that the girl follows protocol. Absolutely she must keep the girl safe.

*

In 1903, a neurologist named Sir Henry Head elected to sever the radial nerve in his left arm for science. He knew that people who experience nerve damage regain sensation over time, and he wanted to map this recovery. What sensations returned first? Second? He and a co-experimenter subjected his left arm to all manner of stimulations over a period of about five years.

If the mother knew about Sir Henry Head's experiment, she would likely say that pregnancy and giving birth had been like severing an important nerve. Seven years later, the mother is still recovering what she lost, only the difference is her experiment is not controlled. There is no mirrored half, like Head's right arm, that preserves her pre-pregnant self.

That she chose to get pregnant, wanted a child, despite all the facts, despite having observed other women in the situation she is in now is a testament to the power of hormones, the mother supposes. Hormones make you do things that are not in your best interest. Hormones are not to be trusted. The problem is you can never be certain when your desires and behaviors are ruled by hormones and when they are not. Perhaps when she wishes the husband were dead, that is hormones. Perhaps the moments she feels tender toward him are the products of hormones. Perhaps when the mother stands at the window and watches the neighbor woman walk out of her house in T-shirt and shorts and sneakers and take off running down the street, no apparent worries about being a woman alone on a street, and the mother longs to abandon the girl and run out after the woman, that is hormones. Perhaps remaining at the window instead of joining the woman is hormones.

*

Although she is not allowed to leave the house, the mother is allowed to blog. In fact, blogging is encouraged. A routine is good, having some sort of work besides cleaning house and rearing a child is good, the husband has said.

The mother is a baker blogger. If you are a baker blogger, you are, de facto, a memoirist. Each new recipe comes wrapped in anecdotes from your life.

There is much the mother cannot share on her blog, of course. Like that the husband is away a lot. Because what if among her readers is a man who sees an opportunity? A mother and child alone. This concern was suggested by the husband, but she shares the same worry, though she'd never admit it to him. His absence makes her nervous, especially at night when she can't see more than a few feet out the house's windows. They have a treadmill in their garage, and often when the girl is in bed at night, the mother considers going out there and running on it, but the garage, though an extension of the house, feels separate from the house. She worries that somehow she'd get locked out there, separated from the girl, and that something terrible would happen.

There is plenty she enjoys about the husband's absence, too. That their bathroom is all hers, for instance. No husband bending over the sink to brush his teeth, a mix of toothpaste and saliva dribbling down his chin into the basin. No mysterious wads of toilet paper on the floor next to the trash bin. No stubble hairs on her bar of soap. But these details she cannot share on the blog, either, for they would embarrass the husband, hurt his feelings.

She does not dare post stories about the girl, either, for there are men who will masturbate to these stories.

So the mother has invented a persona for her blog. The baker of her blog is childless and single. This isn't simply an act of omission: because she does not mention the girl or the husband, ergo, they do not exist. No, the baker in the blog tells her readers she is too selfish to have children, too particular and too hermit-prone to marry. She posts photographs of gorgeous cakes and cookies and writes about how nothing else in life fulfills her the way baking does.

When the mother began the blog, she thought she would blog once a week on Tuesdays. But, quickly, baking and blogging about baking became a necessity. Now she bakes and blogs almost daily. If she can't bake during the day, say the girl is sick, and she must lie next to the girl to keep her company, then she bakes at night when the girl is passed out from a heavy dose of alcohol-laden cough syrup.

They throw a lot of baked goods into the garbage chute.

The mother thinks often of that fairy tale, "Sweet Porridge," about a poor woman and her child who live alone. They have nothing to eat until the child goes into the forest and an old woman gives her a magic pot. When the girl says, "Little pot, cook," the pot makes sweet porridge. When she says, "Little pot, stop," the pot stops. One day while the girl is away, the mother commands the pot to cook and it does, only the mother does not know the command to make it stop. So the pot cooks and cooks until the whole town is buried in porridge. Does the mother drown in all this porridge? The story does not say.

*

As the girl steps out of the bath and the mother presses a towel to the girl's wet hair, the girl says, "I want to cut you open and wear your skin like a house."

The mother plays a game with the girl sometimes, a game she learned from her own mother, in which they use a house as a metaphor for everything and anything that contains, as in a sock is a house for a foot, a lock is a house for a key, a mouth is a house for teeth.

The girl leans into the mother the way she always does after a bath, wraps her wet limbs around the mother. She is so small, so easy to break, and the outside is full of men who wish to break her. Is it any wonder the girl should want to hide in her mother's skin?

The mother worries about the girl's fear. The girl has never played with another child. She has never seen another child except on television or in books. The girl will not know how to be with other people. She will be afraid, suspicious, awkward.

The mother often watches the neighbor—pruning her roses or backing out of the driveway in a car, sunglasses concealing her eyes. The mother once did these things before she got pregnant. She could have chosen to remain un-pregnant, un-mothered, free. She was never comfortable in the world, though. She wonders if this has much to do with why she became pregnant. Maybe it was less hormones, more fear.

What she couldn't have known was that there is plenty to fear in here, too. All mothers must fear at some point that their children may hurt them. That's putting it too mildly. All children do hurt their mothers. They tear their way out of their mother's bodies, after all, unless a doctor cuts into the mother instead of the child's head and shoulders. And then there is the biting of her nipples, the exhaustion when the child cries in the middle of the night, the first time the child hits the mother, the first time the child says to the mother that she hates her or that the mother is stupid or ugly or unlovable. Such injuries are accepted as normal. Children separating their identities from that of the mother, psychologists say, may be cruel. It's a necessary violence.

The mother, being a woman, has come to expect a certain level of cruelty and violence. Like outside, when men on the street have yelled at her, before she got pregnant and left the outside, that she looked like she needed to be fucked. Or when a man on the street grabbed her ass. Or when a man in the office she used to work in would talk over her again and again in meetings. Or when the husband, before he became the husband, told her once that no one else would ever love her like he loves her. A declaration he seemed to think should make her feel loved, but what she heard was that she ought to feel lucky he bothers with her because nobody else would.

Still, there are many moments with the girl when the mother wonders: is this something she should heed? Like when the girl found a small lizard in the house and she made a "leash" for the animal with some yarn and tied it to the coffee table, and the lizard promptly strangled itself.

There are many other moments, having nothing to do with the girl presumably, which also prompt the mother to wonder if she should take heed. The decapitated rabbit head, for instance. The mother must make a choice in these moments: either she takes heed and is afraid and, more often than not, her husband dismisses her fear; or, she does not take heed and risks being guilty of being heedless.

*

The next time the mother hears the thunk of the supply box, she looks out the peephole half-expecting to find another decapitated rabbit head, but instead, there is something a bit larger, rounder, something she can't quite make out through the fisheye lens. Dog shit perhaps.

Protocol does not include anything about unidentifiable-from-the-peephole objects accompanying a supply box.

She takes a breath and opens the door. She sees that the object she couldn't identify through the peephole is a rattlesnake, coiled against the side of the box.

Protocol entails that the mother quickly open the door, quickly drag the supply box into the house, and quickly shut the door. Protocol does not include anything about rattlesnakes.

The mother knows rattlesnakes are not eager to strike, that they do so only when startled or threatened. But quickly dragging the box will surely startle or threaten the rattlesnake.

She shuts the door. She counts to three. She looks out the peephole. The snake is still there.

Perhaps if she drags the box slowly, slowly, the snake will not startle or feel threatened? She could hook the top of the box with the rake from the garage. She could wear boots as she does this. She could wrap leftover scraps of carpet around her legs with duct tape. Perhaps the thickness of the carpet will be enough to prevent the snake's fangs from reaching her skin.

The girl is watching television. She is so entranced that she pays no attention to the mother going in and out of the garage, the noise of the duct tape.

When the mother is finally ready about fifteen minutes later, she opens the door.

The snake is gone.

The mother throws stale macaroons around the box to be sure. No movement. No sounds aside from the thunks of the macaroons.

The mother puts down the rake and quickly drags in the supply box. She quickly shuts the door.

She worries she imagined the snake. She worries about the break in protocol. She worries the snake is real and one among many creatures trying to get inside the house.

She thinks of the tree outside her bedroom. Years ago, when it was a much smaller tree she and the husband brought home from the nursery in a black plastic pot—that pot had been like a diaper the way it held the soil around the tree's roots—she planted the tree closer to the house than she ought to have. She didn't understand then about roots, how far they spread, the damage they can do. She imagines the tree's roots pushing up against the house's foundation, cracking the foundation like cracking an egg into a bowl. Sometimes late at night, when the house is otherwise quiet, she thinks she hears the tree's roots pawing beneath the house.

*

In the fairy tales the mother reads the girl before bed, the monsters are often mothers. Stepmothers, birth mothers, old hags—same difference.

In the horror films the mother watches some evenings when the girl is asleep, the monsters are often children. Adopted children, biological children, little men who are mistaken for children.

The girl is often startling the mother—at night when she wakes from a nightmare and walks into the kitchen while the mother is baking, in the mornings when the mother is drinking coffee and doesn't realize the girl is up. The girl treads silently. No warning. Or like now, the mother walks right by the girl where the girl is curled up on the sofa, and the mother doesn't see the girl until the girl speaks. The mother screams.

After the girl stops crying, she says, "Why did you scream?"

The mother says, "I thought I was alone."

The girl looks confused and also frightened. "Why would you think that?"

*

The husband calls while the mother is licking a thin icing from her fingers. A boiled orange cake is baking in the oven.

The girl is in a television trance. The mother thinks that perhaps the television has sucked the girl out of her body, that the girl's body is an empty husk, the way she sits so still, eyes fixed. A television is a house for a girl, she thinks. But then the girl laughs at something on the screen, and the mother is assured the girl is still snug inside her own skin.

Instead of immediately giving the phone to the girl as she often does, the mother tells the husband about the rattlesnake and about what the girl said about wanting to slit her open and wear her skin.

The husband says, "She says funny stuff, doesn't she? Have you followed protocol?"

The mother says, "I couldn't follow protocol precisely when the rattlesnake was next to the supply box. I had to close the

door and come up with a plan for how to get the box. So I had
to open the door twice that morning. I had to let the box sit for
a bit outside."

The husband says, "Hmm..."

The mother says, "What could I have done differently?
Offered a leg for the snake to bite?"

The husband says, "Nothing like this all these years and
then a rabbit head and then a snake. It doesn't seem possible."

The mother says, "Are you calling me crazy?"

"I'm saying it's probably nothing. There's nothing to worry
about."

"It's been five weeks now. When are you coming home?"

The husband says, "You know I don't know. And even if I
did, I couldn't tell you."

The mother says, "I don't want to live like this anymore."

"What does that mean?"

"I might as well not even have a husband."

The husband says, "Well, maybe I'll die on the job, and
you won't have a husband anymore. And then you'll get a fat
insurance check. Won't that be nice?" The husband laughs.

*

There are two types of baker bloggers. First, there are the bakers
who invent. They create brand new sweets the world has never
tasted before. Or they reinvent classics, making them truly
their own—revamped recipes you could not possibly confuse
with the originals. These baker bloggers are rare. Second, there

are the bakers who purport to be inventors, who present recipes as their own despite that said recipes are entirely generic. They get away with it perhaps because their readers aren't concerned with originality. They just want a good recipe made easily reproducible by beautiful photos and clear instructions. This is the most common type of baker blogger. The mother is neither of these types. She is a baker who bakes other people's recipes, classic recipes, without pretending she has made them her own.

The mother would like to invent recipes of her own, but she doesn't feel ready yet. There is still so much she hasn't made. There is still so much to learn. The idea of wasting ingredients on failures causes her stress. Worse: What if she were to present to the world something as her own that is not?

Someone with the username BlackEyedSue comments on the mother's blog one evening: "Why do you only ever bake other people's recipes?"

The mother writes back, "I'm apprenticing."

BlackEyedSue writes, "This blog is six years old."

*

The husband has been gone 39 days when the girl says, "I want to die."

When the mother asks her why, the girl says, "Because I'm a horrible, horrible girl."

The mother is quiet. She thinks of the lizard. She thinks of her own flesh sliced open like a baked potato. Then she says,

"You are a wonderful girl. And nobody is perfect. We all do things we're ashamed of. Did you do something you're ashamed of?"

The girl repeats, "I want to die." Then she says, "I want everyone to die. I want the whole world to die."

The mother feels sad and scared and, strangely, the tiniest bit proud. The girl has always been a smart, sensitive child. The mother has always taught the girl to express her emotions. And who hasn't felt this way at some time or another?

On the other hand, is this one of those moments in which she ought to take heed?

She worries about her culpability. She loves the girl, but she has never enjoyed playing with her. Playing with the girl is, in fact, almost the worst way to spend her time that she can imagine. When the husband is home, she'll say to him, you play with our daughter, and I'll do these dishes. The husband thinks he is getting the better deal. The mother thinks she is getting the better deal.

At night when the mother takes the girl to bed, the girl clings to the mother like she's all that's keeping the girl from falling from a steep cliff. Perhaps the girl does not feel secure. Because the mother so clearly prefers baking and chores to playing with the girl.

When the mother does spend time with the girl, it is usually to watch movies, and usually she has wine in hand because the movies her daughter enjoys are mostly boring, and even if they're not boring, the mother has watched them with the girl five times already.

Also, the mother frequently zones out while the girl is talking. Sometimes the girl catches her. "Mama, did you hear what I said?"

Just that morning, this had happened. Instead of listening to her child, the mother had been thinking about how she misses orgasms. She is perfectly good at delivering them herself, sans the husband. The problem is the girl is in her bed every night now. She won't even start the night in her own bed. The mother could take a vibrator to her child's bedroom or the hall bathroom, lock the door and be done within a few minutes, but the idea of masturbating in either of these locations is wholly unappealing. The most appealing location for masturbation, other than in the privacy of her own bedroom, is the sofa under a throw while she reads a book or watches television. But there's no way to lock her bedroom from the outside to ensure the girl does not come out.

The mother says, "Well, I certainly hope you don't die any time soon."

This is true, but the mother considers that there would be some consolation in being able to leave the house, in being able to mourn outside in the sunshine and the fresh air.

*

That evening while the girl is in the bath, the mother stands at the window and watches the woman next door throw a stick across her lawn to a small, brown dog. The mother has never seen the dog before. The woman must have brought it home that very day. The mother thinks of the woman driving to a shelter, walking from her car to the shelter, choosing whatever dog she wants.

The dog fetches the stick, but the dog does not bring the stick back to the woman. The dog has not yet learned this game. The woman has to run after the dog and take the stick from its mouth. She throws the stick again. She calls to the dog. The mother hears the woman calling, "Muffin! Muffin!"

The mother taps the glass then. She imagines her and the woman smiling and waving at each other, but the woman does not turn. The mother taps harder. The woman does not turn.

Then the girl taps the mother's hip, and the mother startles. She falls backward into the console table next to the window. Her thigh strikes the corner of the table, forming a bruise that turns blue-black by morning.

*

There is no more sugar or wine in the cupboard. No more eggs in the refrigerator. The stock of toilet paper, dish soap, coffee, yogurt, chicken broth, oatmeal, hand cream, frozen mangos, coconut oil, waxing strips, and sea-salt truffles is low. Although supply boxes are easy to order and always arrive promptly, the mother has never allowed her stocks to get so low before ordering reinforcements. Some part of her has never fully trusted that she'd be able to get what she needed when she needed it. And with the husband away and impossible to contact, what would she do if a box didn't arrive?

There is a grocery store barely two miles away. The woman next door shops there. The mother knows because sometimes the woman forgets her cloth bags and removes from the trunk of her car paper bags bearing the store's name.

The mother no longer owns a car. If there were an emergency that required immediate medical care, they would call paramedics. If necessary, the paramedics would take the mother and the girl to the hospital. There is a phone number engraved into a locket hanging from the mother's neck. Even if the mother were unconscious, the paramedics would open the locket and call the number. It is an emergency number to be used only in an emergency. A stranger, not the husband, would answer and would notify the husband immediately, at which point he would either return immediately or make some other preparations to make sure the mother and the girl are looked after, kept safe.

Running out of food and no supply box arriving: would that constitute an emergency, when a grocery store is just a couple miles away?

As she makes a list of the items they need, she pictures the rabbit head; the rattlesnake; tree roots like fingers scratching underneath their house, poking at the foundation.

The scariest movie the mother ever saw was Hitchcock's The Birds. What made it so scary was its lack of explanation for why the birds attacked.

*

When the husband calls, she does not tell him about the girl's latest talk of killing her and the entire human population. She hands the phone to the girl.

While the girl talks to the husband, the mother studies her list. Should she order pistachios and finally tackle a baked Alaska, the dessert she's been most intimidated by all these years—the one that she'd told herself would be the finale of her apprenticeship? Because if she could manage to seal in the semifreddo with a sturdy barrier of meringue and torch the ice-cream cake without creating an oozing mess, she could do anything, couldn't she?

She hears the girl say, "I didn't see the snake." Then, "She was banging on the window last night."

The mother takes the phone from the girl. "What are you doing?" she says to the husband.

"I just asked her if you guys had seen any more rattlesnakes," he says. "I just wanted to know how you two are doing, just making sure you're both OK."

"Just," she says. Then the mother tells him about how the other day the girl said she wanted the mother to die.

The girl looks at her feet.

"Children don't have much of a filter," the husband says. "I bet you've wished sometimes I'm dead. You just don't say it. Oh, wait: You have."

The mother says, "I never said that."

"Perhaps not so directly."

"She said she wished everybody in the whole world was dead."

The girl starts crying.

"Angela," he says. "She's six." Then, "I can't make any promises, as you know, but there's a good chance I may be home within the week. Maybe much sooner. I can't say for sure, though, as you know."

She says nothing.

"Did you hear me?"

She hangs up the phone, turns off the ringer.

She puts her arm around the girl, says to her, "Everything's OK." She gives the girl one of the giant almond horn cookies with sprinkles she'd made the day before. Then, while the girl watches television, the mother eats three.

*

She puts in her order for a supply box, schedules it for dusk because she has never scheduled a supply box for dusk and so she surmises that whoever or whatever is menacing her will be caught off guard.

Twenty minutes before the box is to arrive, the mother paces near the front window. She watches the woman next door pull into her driveway. Another car pulls in behind her car. A man steps out. He is tall and handsome and wearing a forest green pullover sweater. The husband owns a sweater much like it, only his is more blue. Or maybe not. The more she considers the color of that sweater, the less sure she is of the color.

The mother thinks it can't be cold enough out to warrant a sweater, not when so few of the leaves have fallen from the trees. This makes her think she doesn't like this man. The way the man stands there waiting for the woman to walk to him bothers her, too. Even the way he puts his hand on her arm, like he's laying claim.

The mother watches them disappear into the house.

Five minutes before the box is to arrive, the mother leans over the back of the sofa to kiss the top of the girl's head. The girl smells like popcorn.

*

When the mother hears the thunk of the supply box, she is in position. She takes a deep breath. She leans into the peephole.

She almost makes a sound but quickly covers her mouth. There is a man at her door or at least she thinks the figure is a man. She neglected to turn on the porchlight, and it's just dark enough out now that the figure is more silhouette than flesh. His feet blend in with the supply box, so that his calves appear rooted.

The lights are off on the inside of the house as well, so she knows that even if the fisheye lens were large enough that he could see more than her eyeball through its opposite end, all he could possibly see now is blackness.

She breathes quietly. Watches the figure lean in, too, until he is so close that his head blocks out the faint traces of sunlight.

Is he pressing himself against the door?

She places her palm against the door, then her entire body. She wonders if she might feel the figure's breath and his blood pumping if she listens with her whole body.

When the knock comes, it reverberates through her bones. A code she tries to decipher.

The knock seems to emerge at the small of her back, to thrum there.

Another knock. Only this time the knocking seems to be coming from both the door and from behind her.

She realizes that what she feels at the small of her back is not the knock that moves through the door and into her bones, but a finger. The girl's finger.

"It's me," a voice whispers, but whether it comes from the outside or from the inside, she isn't sure.

The mother stiffens. If she stands very still, maybe no one will know she is there.

Michelle Ross is the author of the story collections *There's So Much They Haven't Told You* (Moon City Press 2017), winner of the 2016 Moon City Press Short Fiction Award and Finalist for the 2017 Foreword INDIES Book of the Year Award for Short Stories.

Her fiction has appeared in *Alaska Quarterly Review, Colorado Review, The Common, Epiphany, Electric Literature's Recommended Reading, TriQuarterly,* and other venues. Her fiction has been selected for Best Microfictions 2020 and the *Wigleaf* Top 50 2019, as well as won prizes from *Gulf Coast* and other journals.

She is fiction editor of *Atticus Review* and was a consulting editor for the 2018 Best Small Fictions anthology.

A native of Texas, she received her B.A. from Emory University and her M.F.A and M.A. from Indiana University. She currently lives in Tucson, Arizona, with her husband and son. She works as a science writer.

This book would not have been possible
without the hard work of our staff.

We would like to acknowledge:

GINNY EGGERTON   Managing Editor
REBECCA BURKE   Assistant Managing Editor
LINDLEY ESTES   Assistant Managing Editor
KYRA KONDIS   Assistant Managing Editor
KILLIAN MOORE   Editorial Assistant
LINDA HALL   Operations Assistant
ALEX HORN   Marketing Assistant

SCOTT BERG   Publisher
GREGG WILHELM   Editorial Advisor
MEGHAN McNAMARA   Media & Marketing Advisor
DOUGLAS LUMAN   Art Director

STILL
HOUSE
PRESS